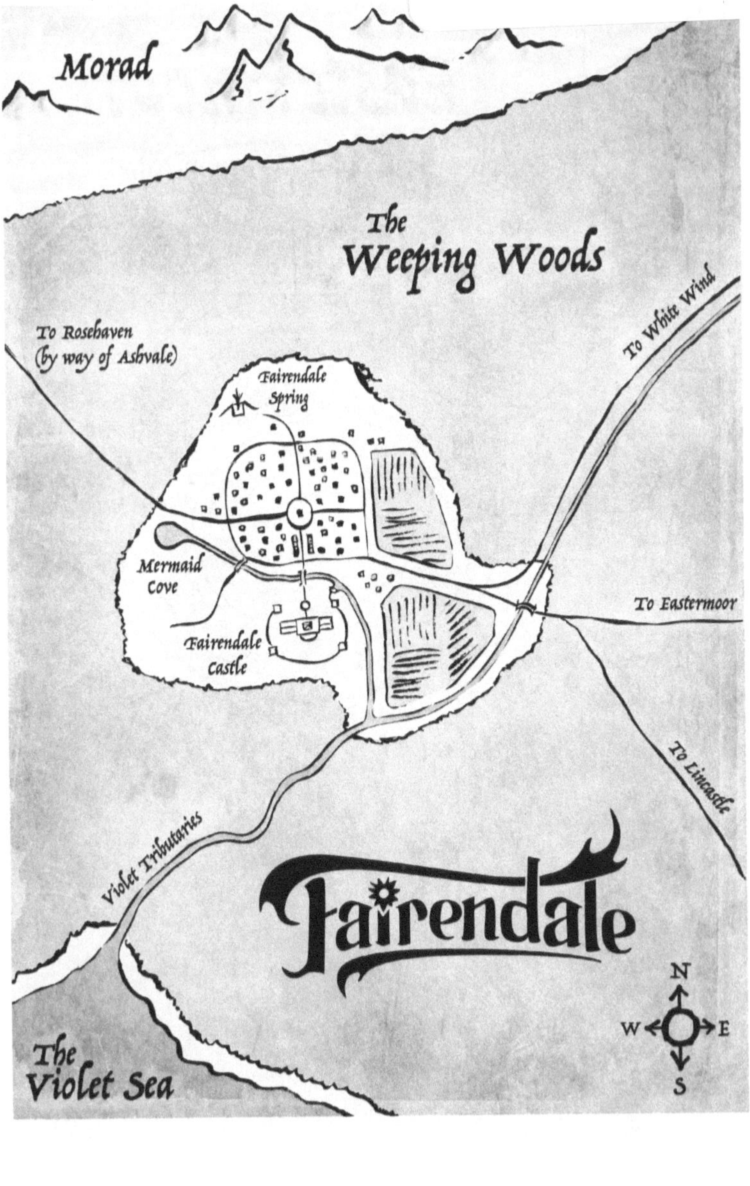

Morad
The Weeping Woods
To Rosehaven
(by way of Ashvale)
To White Wind
Fairendale Spring
Mermaid Cove
Fairendale Castle
To Eastermoor
To Lincastle
Violet Tributaries
Fairendale
The Violet Sea
N
W
E
S

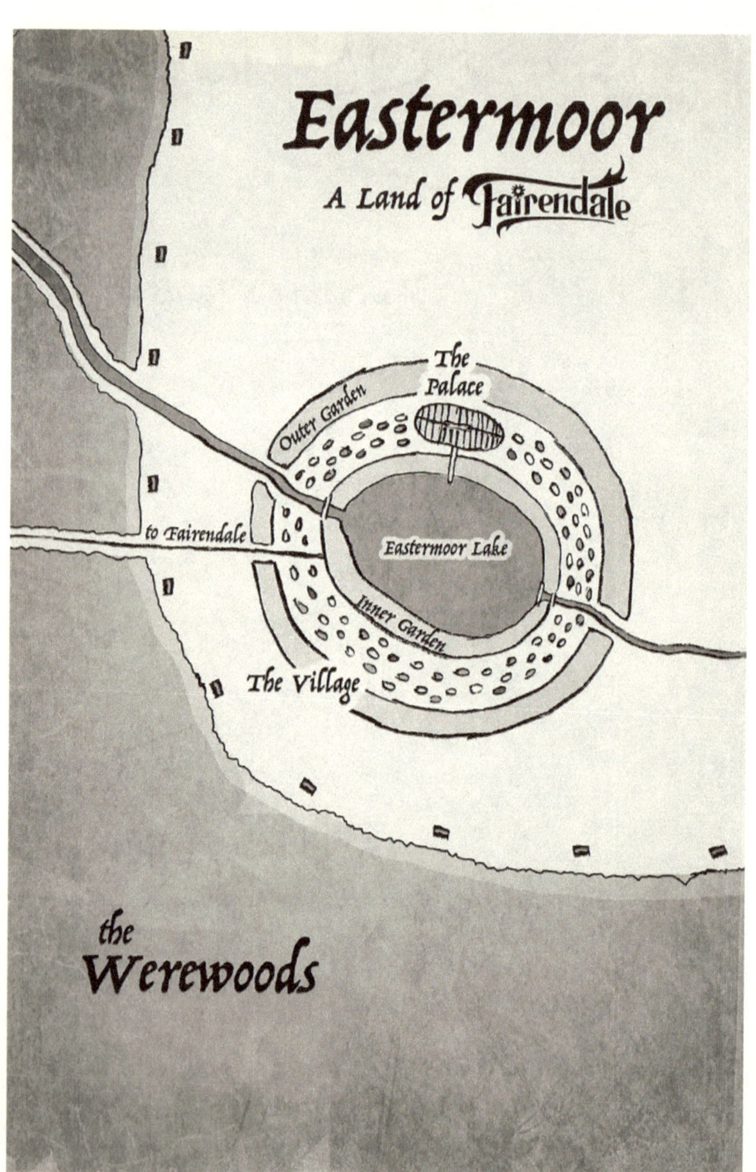

Eastermoor
A Land of Fairendale
The Palace
Outer Garden
to Fairendale
Eastermoor Lake
Inner Garden
The Village
the Werewoods

Fairendale

14

THE GIRL WHO
BEFRIENDED
ROSE-RED

# Read all the books in the Fairendale series!

Book .5: *The Good King's Fall (a prequel novella)*
Book 1: *The Treacherous Secret*
Book 2: *The King's Pursuit*
Book 3: *The Perilous Crossing*
Book 4: *The Dragons of Morad*
Book 5: *The Fiery Aftermath*
Book 6: *The Mysterious Separation*
Book 7: *The Boy Who Spun Gold*
Book 8: *The Boy Who Robbed the Rich*
Book 9: *The Girl Who Awakened the Beast*
Book 10: *The Boy Who Became the Wolf*
Book 11: *The Girl Who Built the Tower*
Book 12: *The Boy Who Loved a Swan*
Book 13: *The Woman Who Stole the Throne*

## Collector's Editions:

Books 1-6: *The Flight of the Magical Children*

## To see all the books L.R. Patton has written, please click or visit the link below:

www.lrpatton.com/writing

L.R. PATTON

# THE GIRL WHO BEFRIENDED ROSE-RED

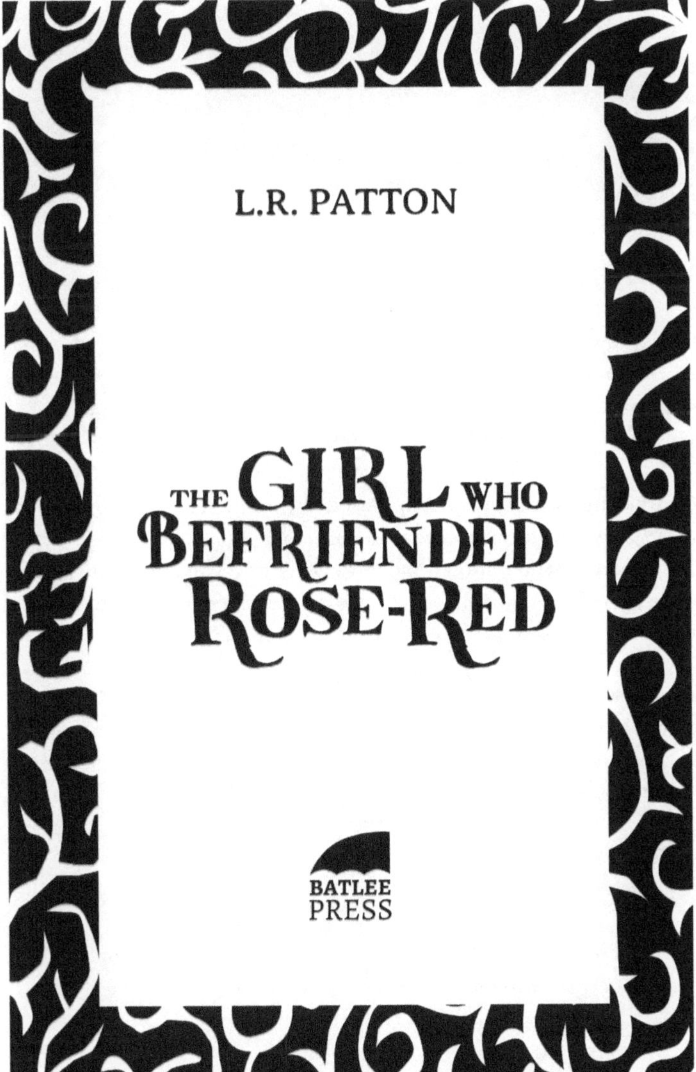

BATLEE PRESS

Published by
Batlee Press
Post Office Box 591596
San Antonio, TX 78259



The author appreciates your taking the time to read her work. Please consider leaving a review wherever you bought it and telling your friends how much you enjoyed it. Both of those help get the book into the hands of new readers, which is incredibly important for authors. Thank you for your support.
www.lrpatton.com

Names: Patton, L.R., author.
Title: The girl who befriended rose-red / L.R. Patton
Description: First edition. | Batlee Press, Texas:
Batlee Press Books, 2019

10 9 8 7 6 5 4 3 2 1

First Edition—2019

# Surrender

It is mid-afternoon, a steamy time of day in the land of Lincastle, where the Enchantress and Theo the Huntsman have woken from a malodorous encounter with a Bonnacon. They woke in the same clearing where they collapsed, not a hair on their heads touched (though their noses were somewhat sore from the sting of foul air released from the backside of the Bonnacon).

They awoke to find a troll barreled over by the Bonnacon's stench and a dragon egg on the ground near him. They awoke, also, to find that one of the blackbirds caged and situated in a cart pulled by a white mare was gone.

These blackbirds represent the lost children of Fairendale. Every time the Enchantress and Theo hunt one down, the Enchantress turns him or her into a blackbird. It makes them easier to transport, she says. What she really means is that she has never been one who enjoys caging children, especially since she was once a child herself—much more recently than anyone in our story might guess.

Oh, dear. I hope I have not revealed too much.

The Enchantress and Theo the Huntsman do not know what to do with the egg, and they have been discussing this for some time. They no longer notice the pungent smell, the residual remains of the Bonnacon; their attention is diverted elsewhere now.

"Should we wait for it to hatch, or should I go ahead and turn it into a blackbird?" the Enchantress says. She is, to tell the truth, glad that the egg has shown up; the looking ball, which she and the Huntsman have been using on their quest to locate and capture all the lost children of Fairendale, recently deviated in its typical mode of revelation; while every other lost child was shown in his or her transformed state, along with the name of the land to which they traveled by way of a Vanishing spell, this latest capture, revealed by the glass orb, showed, simply, an egg. It confounded both her and the Huntsman; they did not know it was possible to vanish and reappear as an egg.

The Enchantress eyes the egg. At least the looking

ball, which has proven somewhat difficult (in that it reveals only one child at a time and has taken the Enchantress and the Huntsman on a wandering journey that makes absolutely no sense to the Enchantress's orderly mind; already they have visited Lincastle twice, and she suspects they will have to visit the wretched land again), was not leading them astray.

At least. But there is still the matter of this wild goose chase and the Enchantress's increasing exhaustion.

The Enchantress would like to be shown all the children in Lincastle so that she can gather them at the same time. But the ball seems to be playing a game.

The Huntsman has taken so many minutes to answer her question that the Enchantress says, "Well? Did you hear me?"

He shakes his head. "We do not even know what is inside it," he says. As though she could have forgotten this important bit of information.

She grinds her teeth together. When a man over-explains something, as though she has forgotten or was not aware or, worse, is as simple as a young child, it has always made her bristle, as it did her mother before her.

"We should leave it in the cart," the Huntsman says. "Let it be."

"Where it might get stolen?" the Enchantress says.

"There are any number of creatures who might want to steal an egg. A blackbird is nothing. But an egg?"

She realizes her mistake almost immediately. The Huntsman glares at her. "They are not simply blackbirds."

Yes. She knows this. She was merely trying to make a point. From an animal's perspective, birds are not as desirable as an overly large egg.

She does not want to say what she is thinking, which is this: She has protected this cart. She has stretched over it one of the most powerful Protection spells in the magical world, and yet, as they were sleeping—or whatever it was they were doing after the Bonnacon showed up and fouled the place—one of the blackbirds was stolen from the cart.

The Enchantress can tell by the shift on the Huntsman's face that he knows what she says is true. She waits for his anger and prepares her next words carefully.

She has grown testy over these weeks of travel. It is not only the magic and the exhaustion that trails her every step because of her excessive magic use. It is, far more, the maintaining of an illusion. The Enchantress has secrets. They are very difficult to keep.

The Huntsman turns his gaze to the caged birds in the cart. She knows he is thinking about the stolen child.

She has already checked the looking ball; it did not show her the stolen blackbird, but it did show her the next child. She is, like all the rest of the currently captured Fairendale girls have been, an old crone. She is near the woods of Eastermoor, where the Were creatures live. The Enchantress would like to be done there and gone before the next full moon. She has already encountered Were creatures and would like very much to never encounter them again.

She shivers.

A chill moves in from the north. Such a chill is unusual for Lincastle, but the Enchantress is not from Lincastle. She is from Fairendale, which lies in the center of all the lands and lends its name and flagship to the realm, so she does not know to be alarmed by this sudden drop in temperature. She is only glad; she has never liked sweating.

The Huntsman picks up the egg and turns it over in his hands. It is as large as his chest.

The ground gives a violent shake.

"We must leave soon," the Enchantress blurts out. Fear sets her teeth on edge.

The Huntsman looks around him, as though trying to find the source of the shaking ground. "Yes," he says, but he is not paying attention to her or her words.

When he turns his face to her, she can see the alarm, which draws more words from her. "What do you think it is?" Her voice is high, shrill. Fear is contagious. She can feel it crawling up the back of her spine, a cold finger skimming skin.

"I do not know," the Huntsman says. "The land of Lincastle has storms of violent wind and rain. Perhaps it is a spring storm?" He sounds unsure. He sets down the egg. The ground ceases shaking.

"Is it still spring?" The Enchantress thought it was closer to mid-summer. But they have been traveling for so long she might have—has—lost track of time. It seems she has always been on this quest.

"It has been twenty-nine days since the children of Fairendale disappeared," says the Huntsman, as though that will clear up the confusion. It does not. She does not remember when she first left the land of Fairendale, on orders from the king to capture all the lost children of Fairendale after his king's guard attack only served to separate them all and send them running for their lives.

He seems to note her lasting confusion; he says, "I believe it is still spring."

The Enchantress shivers again. "It feels much too cold for spring." Though it did not before, when they first woke.

Perhaps the fetid stench of the Bonnacon warmed the place before.

"It is the sea winds," the Huntsman says, but she can hear a faint tinge of concern in his voice. She knows what it means. He does not know for certain that the sea winds are the source of this chill. The Huntsman does not like uncertainty; neither does she.

The Enchantress looks at the sky, which is a brilliant, mid-afternoon blue. She files through her magic instruction, stored in compartments in her mind. Dark magic makes lands chilly. Perhaps it is spreading over the realm, smothering the warmth.

"We should move on soon," the Enchantress says again, calmer this time. "As soon as we can. To the land of Eastermoor." She picks up the egg now, turning it over in her hands, looking for a crack. But the egg is smooth, cream-colored, with not a single jagged line marking it.

The ground gives another, more violent shake.

The Huntsman stares at the ground, looks at the egg, and lifts his eyes to the Enchantress. "We will move on," he says. "And we will leave the egg."

"But the ball wanted us to have the egg," the Enchantress says. She tries her best to make her voice sound strong and confident, but she is not sure she succeeds. It is so tiresome to play a part. She has never liked questions that cannot be answered.

The Huntsman takes the egg from her and sets it down on the ground. The ground ceases shaking. "Something else does not want us to have it." He picks up the egg. The ground shakes. He sets it down. The ground ceases shaking.

"You see?" he says. He has a gleam in his eye, the kind of gleam that used to infuriate her as a girl. The kind of gleam that says *I am right and you are wrong.*

Well. He is not the one in charge, is he? The Enchantress arranges her voice into the coldest, steeliest, most terrible shape she can manage and, with it, says, "We will take the egg."

"And we will likely die." The Huntsman does not even hesitate with his retort.

"The ball does not make mistakes," the Enchantress says. He will not be able to argue with that; the ball has not led them astray yet, although she cannot answer, either, what purpose an egg has to their quest. But it must have some purpose, or the looking ball would not have shown it.

"Truly?" The Huntsman looks at her now as though she really is a child. This fans her anger. It blazes in her chest. She takes a deep breath and lets it out slowly.

No sense in damaging their trust more than it has

been damaged in the past.

She opens her mouth to speak, but the Huntsman beats her to it. "The ball only shows us one child at a time," he says. "We have traveled to Rosehaven and to Lincastle and to White Wind and to Eastermoor and back to Lincastle. You think that is not leading us astray?" His eyes are balls of blue fire. She wonders if he has been holding this in for much too long.

The Enchantress swallows hard. She does not know if the ball can be trusted. But she has nothing else with which to track the lost children. So she says, "I trust the ball."

"Well, I do not." The Huntsman narrows his eyes. "It is—"

"We have found lost children everywhere it has led us." The Enchantress's voice has thinned out and risen.

The Huntsman gestures toward the egg on the ground. "And what of this?" he says.

The Enchantress lifts her chin. "Likely another child. Waiting to hatch." It is ridiculous; she knows it is ridiculous. A Vanishing spell does not turn a child into a creature that has not yet been born. It has never been done, at least not according to the magical texts.

The Huntsman shakes his head. He looks at the Enchantress for a moment before taking the egg in his hands and walking toward the cart. The ground shakes so violently beneath his feet that he can hardly manage without stumbling. Still he places the egg in the cart with the five blackbirds.

For her.

She presses down the emotion in her throat and blinks her eyes so the water will clear. The ground is steady once again. The Enchantress feels a warmth blast through her. "You see?" she says, feeling giddy about being, in the end, correct.

Is she correct? It does not matter; she will claim it for now.

The Huntsman clears his throat but does not say anything.

The Enchantress fills in the space. "The ball has shown us what to do once more," she says.

The Huntsman glowers at the ground now. "There is still a magical child missing." He meets her eyes, and his are challenging. "Will it show us where he is?"

He. So the Huntsman knows which retrieved child is missing.

She would prefer not to think about this missing child. They found him, he disappeared. It is unfair. She grits her teeth, then says, "Maybe the egg contains the missing child."

"It does not," the Huntsman says. He gives the egg such a withering look that the Enchantress expects to see it burst into flames. "It is something else entirely."

"How do you know?"

"Because I know them all." The Huntsman meets her eyes. "I know that the one who has been taken is the first one we found. Homer."

The Enchantress cannot make sense of her spinning emotions. She cannot decide if not knowing this bit of information makes her weaker than the Huntsman or if the Huntsman has proven himself weaker for knowing the names and identities of every lost child, even with their blackbird skin.

She tries to tell herself it is the latter, but her heart does not agree.

The Graces—watchers of the realm, protectors of the seven kingdoms—skim through the lands in their magical looking ball and finish with the one right outside their woods, not too far from where their cottage sits. "They captured six children, did they not?" says the Grace called Good Cheer, who has skin the color of weak chocolate milk (the kind your mother makes you when she has nearly run out of cocoa—still delicious but more milky than chocolatey), hair in thousands of black braids down her back, and a shining pearl necklace that wraps around her throat. Her skin is marked with flourishes that speak of the healing arts. In her previous life, she was a Healer.

She leans closer to the ball, squinting, as though her eyes are not working properly. And she is, to be fair, one hundred sixty-five years old. She has been a Grace for one hundred thirty-four years. We could not fault her for failing eyes.

But her vision is perfectly fine.

"Six children," says, Mirth, a Grace with earth-colored hair and the same color eyes. "And now there are five."

"And a dragon's egg," says Splendor, the last of the three Graces. She has long, gleaming red hair and sharp green eyes that miss next to nothing. She looks at the other two Graces. "They do not know what they are doing with that egg."

Good Cheer ignores Splendor's declaration. "Do we know anything about this looking ball?" she says instead. "The one they are using, I mean."

Mirth and Splendor exchange a glance and shake their heads.

"Perhaps we should find out something, then," Good Cheer says.

"Perhaps we should step in and help them on their quest," Splendor says. Good Cheer is the unspoken leader of the Graces. This was not a technicality the Graces decided; it was simply a matter of first come. Good Cheer was the first Grace, Splendor was the second, and Mirth was the last. They have formed their circle of three, but it has a slight hierarchy, as though it is not a circle but a triangle, albeit a squatty one. Good Cheer is the top point.

And because they are Graces, because they are not concerned with power or notoriety or anything that matters to the world, this technicality has never bothered Splendor or Mirth. They do, however, both want to use their gifts. And Good Cheer is the one who hinders them. For good reason, they know, but still. They are growing restless with their existence: rise in the morning, check the looking ball, talk in their cottage, take a nap, talk more in their cottage, check the looking ball, go to bed.

It would be nice to be needed.

Good Cheer does not answer Splendor, so Splendor tries again. "They are missing a child, and that is a devastating thing to the realm, is it not? Will the looking ball show them a lost child twice?"

Good Cheer shakes her head. "We must trust that it will, for now. We have other things with which to concern ourselves."

Splendor and Mirth look at one another. They have been waiting for such a very long time, and the realm is in such disrepair, such danger. They would like to see it restored sooner rather than later—particularly where the Grim Reaper is involved. Good Cheer seems to think he has sinister plans to begin reaping where he is not permitted, to begin building an undead army, to begin… what? Stepping into the world of the living? How is such a thing possible?

They cannot let it happen. They cannot let their questions be answered. They must step in.

The problem is that in the realm of Fairendale, Graces are only permitted one major intervention—a quest, so to speak—per fortnight, and then they are knocked out so completely that they cannot even observe what their intervention has done until they have woken from their deep sleep. (They are, of course, permitted unlimited intervention in smaller matters—such as swaying the minds of people (provided those people's minds are open, rather than closed), allowing a Prophet to See a Vision (provided he is not completely blind in both sight and his prophet Sight), or guiding a fearsome creature of the woods away from a lost child (they have done this time and time again since the children of Fairendale fled into the forests). They cannot raise anyone from the dead, and they cannot See the future, only the present.)

They must choose wisely when to stage a major intervention and when to let matters go.

Clearly Good Cheer does not think this is a time for intervention.

"I believe much more is coming," Good Cheer says.

"But not much can happen in a fortnight," Splendor says.

"I beg to differ," Good Cheer says. "I died and rose again in fewer days than a fortnight. King Sebastien marched to Fairendale and stole the throne in less than a fortnight. The Grim Reaper has become much more substantial in the last fortnight."

Splendor and Mirth look at her and then at the floor.

In order for a Grace to intervene in the happenings of the realm, all of them must be in agreement that this is the wisest intervention to make. Graces see only what is happening at present and can merely hope that their intervention will do some good. But this means that caution is a wise practice to have. Caution and planning.

Mirth and Splendor are of a different mind; perhaps

they could intervene once every fortnight, set things to right. Only for the time being, while the realm seems in such fantastic disarray.

They suggested as much to Good Cheer. She, of course, disagreed. They reminded her that they could have intervened a fortnight ago and rounded up all the lost children of Fairendale themselves. Good Cheer reminded them that Graces are not to be too heavy-handed. They must allow the people a place, too. Humanity is not humanity without free will.

It is all up to interpretation. This is what makes the purpose of the Graces so maddening—to them, most of all.

"Our colors are fading," Splendor says into the tense silence.

"We are fading," Mirth says.

They look at each other, and it is true. The rich green of their attire and the glistening gold flourishes marking their dresses are beginning to lighten and dull.

"How do you know when it is time to move?" Splendor says. "When we have lost our brilliance completely?"

"We will never lose our brilliance completely," Good Cheer says. "We are Graces." But she is uncertain, and her sisters know it.

"Perhaps if we merely try," Mirth says.

"It is not yet time," Good Cheer says, the same words she always says.

"But how do you know?" Splendor says.

Good Cheer's shoulders sag. She tugs on her pearl necklace. She looks smaller than she ever has before. Are they shrinking as well? "I do not know," she says at last. "I only know what I feel."

"And we feel it is time to move," Mirth says. She looks at Splendor, as though for support, but Splendor is looking at Good Cheer.

"I do not know what I feel," Splendor says. Mirth's mouth drops open. They have taken to talking long into the night, after Good Cheer has gone to bed. They had both been ready, had both agreed to nudge Good Cheer into action.

"Here is what I know," says Good Cheer into the even tenser silence. "Here is Lincastle." She calls up the land on the looking ball. "There is a dragon egg and an Enchantress and a Huntsman who know what they are doing for now. They keep away the creatures and ensure the safety of the lost children." The ball flickers and shows them a snow-covered land. "Here is Guardia, where the snow is coming up from the ground. I do not yet know what this means, only that it means danger."

The ball flickers again, and Fairendale castle rises up from the green haze. "Here is Fairendale, with a monster sitting on the throne."

The ball goes dark. Good Cheer lets the silence shift and swell around them until she says, "It was not supposed to be like this. That is what I know."

The sisters stand there in silence. After a time, Good Cheer retreats to her room, which has been happening more and more of late. Mirth and Splendor look at each other. Mirth feels shame burning her cheeks.

"Give her time," Splendor says. "We cannot fight amongst ourselves. It would not do for the Graces. If we cannot be who we are, then what is the hope for the rest of the realm?" Splendor puts her hand on Mirth's arm. "We must be unified in all things."

Mirth nods.

She will wait. It is all she can do for now. She knows —she feels—that a time is coming when they will be sent over the edge and the only thing that will remain is for the Graces to step in and do their work.

And then sleep.

Blindell paces the land around the border of Morad.

Where is the woman? She sent a message, on the wind, which whispered that she would bring the prince to see him. Or had he misunderstood?

He has been planning the prince's death for an hour or more.

She has not come as she said she would.

Should he venture into the Weeping Woods or take to the sky? He steals a glance at the dragons of Morad. Most of them are stretched out for their daily nap. But every now and again one or two of them look in his direction, as though surreptitiously observing him. He narrows his eyes at their underhanded surveillance. As if he does not know they watch.

As if he does not know he is not trusted.

It is what happens when your father is from a foreign land—a land said to be the home of savage dragons. Blindell feels the fire gathering in his throat. He would likely belong there more than he belongs here. Perhaps he should run away.

But the woman. The prince. Revenge.

He turns his gaze to the woods, his eyes hardly more than red slits.

He feels the eyes of the dragons. He must work very hard not to turn around and roar at them. He walks along the edge of the woods, trying not to arouse their suspicion. The woman has been invisible each time she has visited. They likely will not be able to see her once she shows up today.

If she shows up.

He must have misunderstood. And this stirs the embers of his anger again.

He will go look.

No, he must stay. He glances back at the dragons. They would likely send someone after him, and he cannot risk their discovery. He cannot risk anyone upsetting his plans.

Blindell wonders, briefly, why the dragons are not more accustomed to his strange behavior. He has primed them well, or so he thought, with his outbursts and his angry pacing. He has not been a stranger to the tantrums that define young dragons, and it would be convenient if the dragons of Morad would believe that this—his angry pacing—is just another of them.

But still they watch.

Blindell feels the heat pulsing in his belly. He will show them all in the end. Oh, yes he will.

His agitation is palpable; Blindell has trouble concealing it. The more minutes that tick by, the larger and more cumbersome it grows. The dragons' eyes never leave him, it seems. He has no freedom here. How does one live without freedom?

And now he has a rider. He is not free. He is beholden.

He glares at the mark on his leg, the same mark he must have given the woman. It is a deep gash, but he will survive. Which means she, too, will survive, and he will have to be more careful next time.

Next time…what? Next time he sees the woman? Next time she comes asking him for a favor? Next time she humiliates him with her lack of fear and trembling in the presence of a mighty dragon?

Blindell huffs out a breath, and a smoke ring escapes his nose. It is arranged in the form of a blackbird. He flicks his tail into its center, effectively scattering the image.

Would he be free if he returned to the land of his father? Would they even know him? He has never been there. He knows practically nothing of its dragons, only what his mother told him, so many years ago: they were the most dangerous dragons in the land.

He would like to be one of the most dangerous dragons in the land.

But would he really?

Well, what can he do here? He is still an outsider. He will be an outsider wherever he goes. He is next in line for the throne of Morad, but Zorag has left his council in charge while he is gone, not Blindell. Blindell does not know what that means—that Zorag does not trust him to lead? That someone else will be king? That Blindell will always remain an outsider?

He does not know where the land of his father is. No one has ever told him its location or even its name. Perhaps they do not want him to find it. Perhaps they fear he will become more dangerous than he already is. Perhaps they want to hinder his becoming who he was meant to be.

Blindell gazes up into the sky. He could find them. He is sure of it. He knows of the other dragon lands; he would simply have to fly to them, search them, inquire after his father's relatives. If he left Morad, he could track down what family remains—if family remains at all.

It would be good to escape Morad. And the constant, watching, distrustful eyes.

But then he would not get his revenge. And the anger eating away at his belly would continue its eating. Revenge is the only thing that can cure it.

He will have his revenge.

After several more minutes of pacing back and forth along the line between the lands of Morad and the Weeping Woods, Blindell begins to wonder if he should try to find the prince himself. The woman must have changed her mind. It is what humans do. They make promises and they break them.

The fire within him surges.

He will do it.

He will find the prince.

He will destroy the land of Fairendale as its king destroyed his family.

Blindell lifts into the sky, his wings sure and strong.

Another dragon lifts into the sky as well, but Blindell pays him no mind; he does not need dragon sitting, as the dragons of Morad seem to believe. Why do they watch him so closely? Why is he being followed? If his cousin, Zorag, were here, they would pay Blindell no mind. They would be too busy fawning over their king. Blindell had always been ignored by the dragons of Morad, in the presence of Zorag. And now...

They underestimated him. But he will show them all.

The anger makes him fly faster.

"Blindell!" A voice reaches out to him. He does not stop flying, but he turns his head. It is the dragon Larus, whose scales might match the Fairendale sky if the sky were not a permanent gray now. He does not look nearly as majestic as he would if the sun were shining, illuminating his skin with a shimmering light.

"Go away," Blindell says.

"Where are you going?" Larus says. His green eyes are fixed on Blindell, but Blindell turns his face away.

"It is no concern of yours," he says.

"You must return," Larus says.

"You are not my king," Blindell says. "You cannot order me to do anything."

"The council has—"

"The council means nothing to me." Blindell's voice is a loud rumble, and fire chases his words. Larus has caught up with him. Blindell is careful to aim his fire away from Larus; he is not foolish enough to believe he could get away with a small air attack. The dragons of Morad are small in number, but they are far greater than he is alone.

"We have our laws," Larus says, and the words seem to hold a threat.

Blindell flies harder.

Larus keeps up.

Blindell's eyes catch on the woods. They are much darker than they were even days ago. They look like a spot of black ink has been spilled and is soaking into all the trees. He slows momentarily, then stops, hovering in the air. Larus hovers in the air beside him, seemingly unaware of the woods and their stain.

But Blindell knows the dragons of Morad are never unaware of anything.

Why did they not tell him?

Larus wastes no time getting to his point. "I know that your roots were forged in a different land and that perhaps you do not inherently understand the ways of dragons and people."

Blindell feels the anger pressing into a ball in the back of his throat, blocking off his words. Larus continues. "But I assure you that the way we conduct ourselves, the decisions we make, the actions we decide to take, are best for both dragons and humans."

Words finally tear from Blindell's throat. "I am not a foreigner," he says. "I have lived among you all my life. My mother was a dragon of Morad."

"Yours is a young life." Larus's voice is gentle. Blindell moves forward again, but his progress is slower. He has lost his quickening anger and has been overcome with a slackening sadness.

Larus follows his every move, like an unwanted shadow. He has never known Larus to be so persistent. He has known him only to be a coward.

Blindell almost tells him this when Larus says, "You must come back."

"There is no must," Blindell says. "You have no

power over me." And it is at this exact moment that something astonishing happens. Blindell falls from the sky. He tries to stop himself, but his wings do not work. He turns head over tail in a line directly back toward Morad. He sees it happening, but he is powerless to stop it.

He crashes to the ground in the center of what seems like every dragon in the land. All eyes are on him. He cannot move.

The council members crowd around him. Larus; the ancient red dragon Alvah, whose scales have faded to a dull orange-red; the more ancient dragon Oned, whose scales are gray, almost colorless, and peeling off in places; and the young red dragon, Malera, who was like a mother to him after his own mother was killed during the Great Battle.

Even Kohar, the old pale yellow food gatherer who rarely ever rises anymore (and certainly does not hunt—Blindell does that for him), has made an effort. His eyes are milky but still a lovely shade of blue.

"Blindell." Malera says his name as though it holds all the disappointment in the world.

Blindell still cannot move, but he can speak, and what he says is, "My cousin will never love you."

Malera's eyes are the only part of her that registers

the sting of his words. Blindell does not feel satisfied, however; he only feels worse. Malera says, "We have our expectations, our laws. You are breaking them."

"My cousin put me in charge while he was gone," Blindell says. He has told himself this so many times that he has practically convinced himself it is so, that the dragons have taken away this responsibility meant for him.

"He put us in charge." The voice is musical, a human's voice, not a dragon's. A woman steps out from behind Oned. She has golden hair and a smooth face but sapphire eyes that say she has lived many more years than her hair and face register.

The woman holds herself like a princess, her back straight, her neck long, her chin tilted slightly. In her hands is a staff of almond-colored wood. It tapers to a point at its bottom, and its top bears iron claws that curve around a ball of crystal.

A sorceress. What is this?

Blindell has never seen this sorceress before, but he has sensed her.

He still cannot move. The woman walks closer.

"Who are you?" Blindell manages to spit out.

"I am a protector," she says. "I have come to protect you." She walks in a slow circle around him, her staff tapping the ground every few steps. Blindell tries to snap at her, but his face slams into a very hard wall.

He can move now, so he stands and lunges toward her. The wall he cannot see holds him back. He touches it, slides along its curving shape. It is an invisible prison. Blindell roars, a sound that holds all the anguish and anger crumpled up inside him.

When he is finished, Malera says, "We tried to warn you." Her voice is soft, gentle, soothing. "And now we have done what we thought we must do."

"Let me go!" Blindell rams the wall again and again, but every time he tries another escape, the wall knocks him off his feet. At last, he does not get back up.

It is a magic circle. He knows about magic circles. They keep threats contained. They are complicated spells, and he has never encountered one. Now he is in one. He is contained. The woman raises a hand, and Blindell feels his body lift and tilt. He is on his feet again. But he cannot move, once again.

"What have you done?" he says.

"What I must," the woman says. "To protect you and all of us." She extends her hand behind her, gesturing to the throng of dragons. Her eyes lock with Malera's. Malera nods.

Blindell is a dragon statue. There is nothing he can

do. He opens his mouth to find that even his words do not come. She has taken everything from him.

The cold sting of betrayal slides down his spiked back.

It is the woman. The red-haired one, his rider. He knew there was no way to trust a human being. It is she who has put him in this magic circle that binds him, and he will never trust another human being again.

Even though the woman standing before him has golden hair and sapphire eyes, the only woman Blindell sees is the red-haired, green-eyed one.

He will have his revenge in the end.

They will all see.

The golden-haired woman turns around, and the dragons with her. They walk together, toward the council cave, dragons flanking her miniature side.

She disappears from view long before the dragons do.

Rose has been wandering around the woods near Eastermoor for many days. She does not know that these woods are called the Were Woods, coming as she does from the land of Fairendale, but she does know that what she has seen could fill volumes of story books. In fact, she has fashioned some writing material from the bark of a tree, and she has been carving her stories—all of them true!—into the bark. It is a primitive arrangement, but it is the only arrangement she has been able to imagine currently. Rose dreamed of becoming a scribe in the land of Fairendale, before the king's men tore through the town on the command of King Willis, to capture all the children of the village but especially those with magic.

Rose has the gift of magic. She did what any other child in fear for life would do: she ran.

A Vanishing spell transported her to these strange and mysterious woods, which have filled her primitive story books. She cannot wait to return to her homeland and tell her stories, transcribe them to proper texts.

An ache snakes down her chest.

Will she return? She does not know. She does not even know where she is or in what direction Fairendale lies. She is not directionally proficient. Perhaps she should have paid more attention to her mother during geography instruction.

It is too late for regrets, however. Rose glances at her bark books, as she has begun calling them, piled on the ground around her. She has not found a sufficient abode as yet, but she is actively searching. She has sketched one in a bark book, but every time she tries to create it with her magic, it looks nothing like what she envisions. She tells herself it is not the drawing, but she knows better. Art was never her strength.

Rose has created nine bark books in the last twenty-nine days, which is how long she has lived in these woods. Lived is, perhaps, a strong word for it. She has been existing, gathering water from a vertical stream that trickles down a collection of rocks not far from where she sits now; eating bugs, which, even now, turns her stomach; and sleeping beneath the wide open space of sky and stars. She is no survivalist. She will have to think of something soon. No one can exist for long in woods without preparation.

As much as she disliked her brother, Niram, when she shared the same cottage he did, she has, in these lonely days living in woods, found her thoughts returning to him again and again. Niram would have known what to do. He was a survivalist. He was brave. He was daring.

Her mother called Niram reckless, because sometimes he stepped too close to the Weeping Woods or swam in the tributary where the mermaids were said to be or played in the Sleeping Fields on the edge of Fairendale and went missing for an entire day.

Mother had called Rose sensible ("You're sensible, Rose. You know how to trust your instincts and make good decisions. You will make a fine queen someday." Those had been Mother's exact words). But Rose thinks that reckless might work better when lost in the woods than sensible does. After all, Niram's recklessness taught him how to build shelters from sticks and find food in wild grasses. Rose has none of that ability.

She tries to distract herself with the bark books. She reads her observations about these woods. They are as mysterious as they are wild. She saw men shift into hideous beings during the first full moon (she did not watch for long; she was much too frightened of being discovered and, most likely, devoured—or worse). She has seen fairies glowing in the treetops. She has observed creatures for which she has no name.

She never read much about the creatures of the lands, because they frightened her. But somehow, being in these woods, observing, hiding away from probing eyes that wanted her to be something she was not, feels like a sort of freedom. She can sit all day and dream up stories, and no one will tell her otherwise.

It is lonely and yet it is marvelous.

The creatures she has written about have, so far, left her mostly alone, but fear has begun gathering at the edges of her mind. She has been undeniably lucky so far, but luck never lasts forever, does it? She cannot help but feel that her luck will run out at any moment.

Rose has made it her custom to never stay in the same place for long. She has found many freshwater tributaries with monstrous inhabitants. She has seen trolls, reptiles, goblins (from a far distance), mermaids (in their lovely form), and even spirits of those who have gone before. She does not sleep near these tributaries, nor does she even approach them to fetch water; she would be foolish to do so. She has, thus far, gathered water from tiny streams pressed between rocks, a good distance from open water.

Though she has enjoyed this broadening of her mind and imagination, Rose would very much like to return to Fairendale. She has grown weary of the diligence required to record and observe, and, not least of all, remain safe in recording and observing.

But even if she knew the direction in which Fairendale lies, she would not know how to get there. She does not have the kind of magic Mercy and Hazel had; hers is a weaker sort. She does not have the practical planning skills of Ruby and Lina. She does not have the intelligence of Minnie and Dorothy.

Rose was always the most beautiful. And what does beauty matter in a place like the woods?

She did not want to be the most beautiful, of course.

It was something her mother suggested when Rose failed at nearly everything else. "At least you have your beauty," her mother always said. She had no idea that Rose also had her stories. Stories were not an acceptable vocation for a daughter of the Village Elder and his wife. They were grooming her to be a princess.

Rose does not want to be a princess. She wants to be a scribe.

During her first few nights in the woods, her mother's voice bothered and nagged: "Always use an herbal poultice on your face to keep it young and lovely." Rose looked for something that might pass as a poultice, but the first time she laid a foreign leaf, dipped in water, on her cheeks while she slept, her face swelled to significant proportions and itched so badly she wanted to remove her skin. She had not attempted again.

She tries to drown out her mother's instructions with her own words, carved onto bark books.

Rose, today, nearly stumbles over a tree root that rises above the ground like a severed arm. She catches herself before plummeting into a body of water so clear she can see all the way to the rocky bottom.

And there is a monster, staring back at her.

She screeches and scrambles away. One of her bark books drops into the water. She does not even watch it sink to the bottom. She presses her eyes closed and tries to make herself small. Perhaps the monster did not see her.

After some minutes, she opens her eyes. No one is in the clearing. Perhaps she can rescue the bark book. Perhaps she was mistaken.

She peers into the water, and the same monster's face peers back at her. But this time something is different. This time she knows it is her.

She gasps. No! It cannot be. She is old! And wrinkled! And her eyes are the dullest of blues where they used to be so bright her mother said they glowed. And her beautiful hair! She pats the mop of gray, braided and coiled like a crown around her head.

Rose backs away from the water, forgetting all about her bark book, and places a hand over her faltering heart. How will she ever get out of this predicament? She never learned to do a Vanishing spell or a Transformation spell or anything that might serve her well now. Her magic never mattered all that much to her. She wishes she had listened better.

Her mother would be horrified to see her in this condition. And what would her father say? She would be just like Niram: a disappointment.

Her thoughts, now, turn toward the other fleeing

Fairendale children who shared her adventures—escaping from the king, hiding in an underground portal, crossing the dragon lands, hiding once more in an invisible shoe-shaped house. Were they transformed so drastically? Surely none of them have become as hideous as she is.

Rose decides she will cheer herself by making a new dress from magic. At least she knows how to do this; she did it many times in the village of Fairendale, when her mother urged her to look presentable for Prince Virgil. Prince Virgil never even looked her way; he only had eyes for Hazel. He thought no one noticed. But Rose did.

She gathers a few sticks from the ground and touches her polished, glass-like staff to the collection. Her effort produces a colorful, silken fabric. Rose wrinkles her nose. She was trying to produce a dress, not the fabric for it. She lifts up the pile of cloth, which embraces the light of the sun beaming through the trees so it shimmers and sparkles. As soon as she touches it, she feels a mysterious exhaustion pull her into sleep. Magic demands much, especially of those who have not eaten a solid meal, those who have subsisted on only insects, for twenty-nine days.

When Rose wakes, the sun has moved significantly in the sky, turning morning to noon. She has no strength left to move from her marginally comfortable space, and, with nothing else to do, she attempts to turn the fabric, once more, into a lovely dress. She never can get it right, and every time she tries, she falls asleep again. Her magic weakens. She weakens. She assumes it is because she is a very old woman.

In the end, Rose throws out the material, thinking it is much too grand for a woman who looks like she does. She sits on a log and broods, shadows gathering around her as the sun shifts and moves. The voice of her mother reaches her from across the many miles, in a memory of her parents discussing their uncertain economic future: "At least we have Rose. She is so beautiful she will surely help us rise in our situation. We will never be hungry again."

What they meant was that Rose might be beautiful enough to marry the prince. She always held on to that hope, that responsibility, that invitation out of destitution.

And now she does not even have that.

Rose dissolves into tears. She should give up, lie here, and wait for the creatures to come and get her.

Which is precisely what she does.

# Visit

For a very long time, Mira had been waiting for her beloved to return.

This story was twisted and complicated. She had fallen in love with a pirate; he had left her for the rolling seas, with a promise to return.

Nearly forty years later, she was still waiting.

She could not accept that he had died. It was not the way her life was supposed to unfold. Of course she had seen the pirates hang one day, years ago, when she was nineteen and had loved him for only two years. But she could not, still, believe that he had been among those swinging in the briny winds that swept off the sea. Her hope was an undying thing, fluttering in a heart that was reserved for him and only him.

It had been so many years. Hope was but a sliver

now.

Mira lived in a kingdom that was really only a very small island on the other side of the world from Fairendale, completely unknown to the people of Fairendale. The people of Fairendale, too, were completely unknown to the residents of the Varena Isles. It may seem strange that this was the case, but it was not so unusual at the time. Maps were primitive in those days, since many of the explorers sent out to search for new lands and map their progress instead disappeared without so much as a trace. The people, with their limited scientific knowledge, believed that the earth was flat. They believed that their explorers had merely reached the edge of the universe and fallen off into oblivion.

Mira did not live alone. She shared the castle with her father and stepmother, the king and queen of the Varena Isles. But her father had become distant in his old age, and her stepmother, year by year, had become increasingly cold and cruel, likely due to her inability to bring forth a child. Mira wondered, often, what it would be like to leave it all behind and go somewhere else.

But where was there to go?

Her beloved had asked her once if she would sail the seas with him. She had cited her duty, her people, her family. All of it had forsaken her.

She should have gone when she had the chance. Though life on the sea would have been a hard one, it would have been better than life in a lonely castle.

What complicated matters even more was that ever since Mira had fallen in love with a pirate, her father had refused to let her leave the castle. A pirate was no match for a princess, which meant, in his mind, that Mira was not wise or competent enough to choose a husband who would sit beside her on the throne. Mira resented this assumption, of course, but in her land there was nothing much she could do. A woman inherited the throne, it was true, but a father chose her prince.

She was not one, however, to simply sit and acquiesce. When her father introduced her to the parade of eligible dukes and lords and earls, all on a mission to win Princess Mira's hand in marriage, Mira staged her resistance in invisible ways. She once beat a duke at an archery tournament, disguised as a man. She once ate more soup than an earl during an eating challenge. She once wore a bearskin and was the first to find, capture, and return to the castle a monstrous wild boar released in the woods behind the castle for the hunting contest.

She did well enough on her own. She did not need a prince.

And now it had been nearly forty years. Fifty-seven was not considered an old age in Varena; on this island Mira was still well within the ideal marrying years. Time was counted differently in a place where people could live for more than three hundred years.

She felt much older than she was. She was tired. And the loneliness, well.

Mira turned away from her tower window, which looked out on the sea—the awful, dangerous, dream-killing sea. She sat on the edge of her bed. She thought.

A noise in the corner of her room, a small pop, startled her. Before her stood a man. A very old man.

"Hello," he said. Something about his voice set her at ease. It was musical, though timeworn.

She stood.

He reached out a hand, then let it drop to his side. "Forgive me for startling you," he said. He looked up at the walls, the ceiling, the one window scratched out of stone. "Why are you in a tower?"

She shook her head. She still could not speak.

The man studied her for some minutes, as though he were searching for something. At last, he said, "I have come to beg your help."

At that, Mira found her voice. "I am in no position to help anyone." Her voice held so much sorrow she could hardly stand it herself. She glanced at the walls. "I am in a cage."

"If I could release you from the cage, would you help?"

Mira studied the man. She looked at his strange green and yellow eyes punctuated by white eyebrows. She noticed his high forehead, the tufts of white hair covering his ears, the beard pointing to his belly. She saw the hope leaking out of him.

He was a foreigner, but she was not afraid. So she said, "Perhaps."

The man bowed, and when he straightened, his eyes had turned soft. "I have waited many years to meet you, Princess Mira."

Her heart thumped. Could it be?

No, he was much too old. And the eyes were different —green, not the color of rich earth. She breathed for a moment before saying, "Who are you?"

His smile carved out wrinkles in his cheeks and around his eyes and even on his forehead. His entire face smiled. "I am Bregdon, prophet of White Wind, in the realm of Fairendale."

She had never heard of such lands. "Are you an enemy?" she said.

The prophet laughed and shook his head. "I am no

enemy," he said. "I come in peace. But for an important purpose."

"What is that purpose?" she said. She did not dare to hope. She straightened her back and willed herself to think only of this man in her room and not the possibility of escape.

"I need you to accompany me back to the land of Fairendale."

Her resolve crumbled. Her heart hammered, her knees turned weak, her temperature plummeted and rose again, in quick succession. She nearly lost her balance.

Could it be so easy?

But a dark worry eased into her mind. What about her beloved? How would he find her if she left Varena? Would she wait for forty years, only to just miss him with a trip to another land?

The cage. Even if her love returned, she would never be able to see him. And at least, out there, she would be free.

Bregdon mistook her silence for apprehension. "I will sail with you," he said. "I am quite the oarsman." He smiled again, with his whole face.

She smiled back. She liked this man very much.

But there was a problem.

"How will I escape from the castle?" Mira said.

"How did you escape it when you and your beloved met all those years ago?" Bregdon said. He looked as though he knew precisely how she had escaped.

Mira stared at him, and now fear was a tight knot in her throat. How did he know? No one knew. Or, rather, only one knew. And she had sworn secrecy.

"I am a prophet," Bregdon said, and his smile never slipped. He seemed to be reassuring her.

And could he read her mind?

Because Bregdon did not respond to this question that she arranged so carefully in her mind, she knew she was alone with her thoughts. That was something.

"Very well," she said. "I will use the bearskin."

Bregdon nodded.

The last time she had used it, its power had frightened her a bit. It had overtaken her, changed her whole shape. Changing shapes in the land of Varena was considered witchcraft. Witches were hung like pirates.

But she knew there was nothing else to do. She would risk it. She had someone on her side now.

Mira cleared her throat. "What will I do in the bearskin?"

"You will meet me at the docks," Bregdon said. "I know you are familiar with them."

Her face grew warm. But perhaps his mention rattled

something in her, because before she could stop them, out tumbled the words: "He will not be able to find me again." She looked at her feet, clad in silver slippers.

"He will find you," the prophet said. "Someday."

Mira's head snapped up so quickly she heard the crack. The prophet's eyes were shining. He nodded.

"He is alive." Bregdon said the words as though they were fragile, and Mira felt them dance across her heart like tiny glass slippers.

He was alive. He had not been hanged all those years ago.

But why had he not returned to her?

"Oh." She pressed her hand to her mouth. In all her years, she had not dreamed that he would still be alive. She had hoped, yes, but she had not dared to believe it was certainly true.

She was shocked out of her current state by the prophet saying, as though it were an afterthought, "We sail to care for your brother."

"My brother?" Mira said. "But I have no brother."

The prophet stood at her door. His eyes were shadowed now. "There is much you do not know about your father. And this is one of them: he had a son whom he gave away to a sorceress so that his beloved wife might live."

"But my mother did not live." Mira felt the words rattle out of her, a storm of sorrow and anger that had never been tamed in all the years she had been alive. Her father blamed her for her mother's death. And his blame became her blame.

"You have been told otherwise. But your mother lives."

Mira felt the world sliding off-kilter, felt it shifting under her feet, felt it writhe and snag. "Where is my mother, then?" she said. Her words lifted on the air, light and papery.

"She lives in the woods," Bregdon said. His voice, unlike hers, was strong, resolute. "She is a tree."

Mira was surely dreaming. She could not reconcile what she heard with what she knew: a person could not be a tree.

But the prophet did not offer any more explanation about her mother. He said, simply, "You were twins, and your brother is the king of a distant land. He was given to a sorceress at birth in exchange for your mother's life."

Mira wondered, briefly, why it was not her who was given away, until she remembered: she was the heir to this throne.

She opened her mouth to ask something else of the prophet, but he was gone.

And left alone, once more, in the empty room, Mira's anger surged toward her father. She wished she could visit him, but she could not risk suspicion, could not risk ruining her opportunity for escape. So she sat on her bed and ignored all her questions and made her plans.

In the back of her mind, a tiny, desperate sliver of hope began to grow. It began to glow. It began to whisper, *Happily ever after.*

If only such a thing existed.

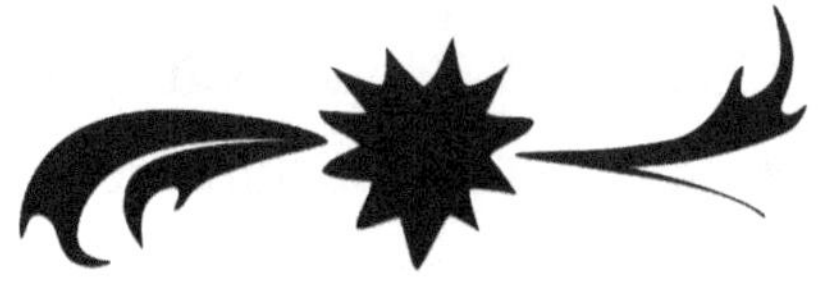

# Doubt

Rose lies on the forest floor for a very long time—
practically all day. It is a wonder no creatures snatch her
up, but she supposes she is much too ugly even for them.

But, as the sun sinks into its mid-afternoon position,
she hears a noise, like that of a beast, and she realizes,
with a start, that she does not want to die here like this.
She scrambles for cover, which, for her, means hiding
behind a tree.

A girl, not a beast, skips into view. She appears to be
dancing with trees. She moves from one of them to
another, her golden-brown hand tracing a circle all the
way around a trunk before she moves to the next. She
stops and looks around, her red hair falling in waves
down her shoulders and back.

"I thought I heard someone weeping," the girl says, as

though talking to someone else. There is no one else with her, at least not anyone Rose can see. She looks to be about Rose's age—or at least the age Rose was before a Vanishing spell turned her ancient.

Her stomach twists.

The girl continues staring into the trees. "Is anyone here?" she says, as though expecting the trees to answer.

Rose feels a longing so deep and wide that she almost emerges. How wonderful it would be to run and skip and dream with another human being. But she knows better. People are unpredictable. Would the girl look at her with terror or disgust? She does not want to know.

So she remains hidden behind the tree. She hardly even breathes.

She thinks that perhaps the girl will move on, so she is entirely surprised when the girl turns toward the tree behind which Rose is hiding—it is a very large tree, and she is sure that no part of her is visible; she is a small old woman, not a large one—and says, in a singsong voice, "Come out, come out, wherever you are."

Rose very nearly does, thinking this girl could be no danger at all, but then she sees a fearsome creature watching the girl from the shadows. It moves closer. It is a massive beast with black brown fur and tufts of hair sticking up in random places. It walks on feet that look like hooves, and tusks curve out from the top of its head.

It could devour both Rose and the girl in one gulp.

The creature creeps closer to the girl. Rose cringes behind the tree, folding herself into the smallest form possible. She is unable to do anything but shake in the most overwhelming wave of fear she has ever known. She cannot move, she cannot call out, she cannot even lift herself to her feet. She is trapped in an invisible cage of cowardice. She tells herself it is self-preservation, to ease her guilt.

The girl skips away, and the beast follows her.

Rose breathes, in, out, in, out. She rises to her feet. She knows what she must do.

She knows, but the bars of fear are thick.

She presses against them and discovers that they give. She slips through them. She follows the girl and the beast. She keeps her distance—as in, she can no longer actually see them—but she *is* following them.

It does not take long to lose them. But Rose tells herself that at least she tried.

Before she can find the girl again—Rose was never much good at tracking, either—she breaks into a grove of trees that grow much closer together than the trees in the rest of the forest. This grove is followed by thick, thorny bushes, which are followed by a collection of plants with brilliant red leaves. Once Rose has conquered each of these barriers, she finds herself standing in front of a large castle. It is made of black stone, which gives it a menacing look. Fog settles at the top of its spires, which rise well above the trees.

It appears abandoned, but Rose does not think it wise to explore. She can feel something strange about this castle. She can feel something…dangerous.

Rose shivers and draws her dark gray cloak tighter around her.

Why is there a castle in the middle of the woods? Woods are not for castles, or at least this is what she thinks she remembers. She was always enamored with castles, and it was the only thing she really paid much mind when her mother was instructing her in geography. She knew all the royal families, knew the number of servants on staff, knew the features and grand characteristics of every castle in the land. This one was not in the books.

In spite of her heart's slamming, the purpose of which is to pull her back toward the woods, Rose ventures closer to the castle. She is drawn by curiosity, something she has not felt in many hours (she is accustomed to a constant curiosity; it is the hallmark of scribes—asking questions, interfering, spying). She pats her pocket for a bark book and brings one out.

She wishes she could sketch this castle, but what she does, instead, is describe it.

Black towers like spears, situated on the left, right, front, and back.

Green moss on the black-spotted gray steps leading up to the entrance.

Windows lined with curtains of an indistinguishable color.

Perhaps, if she ventures closer, she might see inside. Rose takes a step forward. The stone is weathered, as though this is an ancient castle. The closer she gets, the more Rose feels the prickling of unease. This castle does not belong. This castle should not be here.

But still she moves, until she is only a few steps from the stairs that lead up to the entrance.

She stops and stares. It is so large, so dark, so mysterious.

Rose nearly steps onto the first stair when a snap off to her left startles her—a stick breaking, perhaps? Her heart begins an erratic stumble. She looks. She blinks. She closes her eyes for several seconds and opens them again. The beast does not disappear.

He is not looking at her; he is, instead, staring at the spires. But Rose is exposed. It is only a matter of time before he notices her. And this is what freezes her breath, what pulls forth, regrettably, a large and terrified gasp.

The gasp lifts from her body, circles the air, and slams into the solid stone of the castle with an echoing hiss. The beast turns her way. His beady black eyes bore a hole right through her chest.

Rose runs.

She imagines that the beast is chasing her, and this moves her legs much faster for much longer than she normally would manage. When she turns around, no one and nothing is there. She collapses to the ground, her breath heaving in and out in gulps and chokes.

And then she weeps. She weeps for her family and her friends; she weeps for her hunger and her loneliness; she weeps for her future, which she does not think is a very long one, with all these dangers in the woods.

After all, she was never a courageous or clever girl. Only a beautiful one.

And now she has lost even that.

What kind of future awaits a girl who has nothing?

The late afternoon light is somewhat brighter than he would have expected; the trees have thinned out in this expanse of forest. Theo the Huntsman knows that he and the Enchantress, along with the five lost children of Fairendale and the egg in the back of the cart, are somewhere outside the land of Fairendale in the Weeping Woods, which have grown back practically all their leaves and trees since the great fire that raged through them weeks ago. The dragons of Morad were responsible for the fire, though it could very well be attributed to the king's men, who, in their haste to capture the lost children of Fairendale, stepped across the border of Morad and broke the ancient treaty that had been set in place in the days King Sebastien ruled the Fairendale throne. The fire burned everything, but the woods in these lands are good at self-repair.

Theo thinks for a long moment about how he saw his parents and several of the village children running through these woods, back when the king's men invaded the village of Fairendale with the intention of capturing all its children. He saw them in the dragon lands. The dragon lands and the woods that burned.

But he saw Homer and Ruby with his mother and father. So they survived the fire. But why has he not found his sister? Where is his mother? Where is Father?

It is not the first time he has been plagued by these questions.

Theo tries to shake off the wonderings. He and the Enchantress have made good time on their journey from Lincastle. He suspects the Enchantress sped them along, attempting to distance them from the shaking ground. He did the same, with his own secret store of magic, and now he is somewhat exhausted, too.

It is an arduous thing to play a part, hiding things from people. He wishes he could simply tell the Enchantress who he is; she would not even know him, would she? Unless his name has been released. Theo, the magical boy of Fairendale. Theo, the one who caused the capture of Fairendale's children. Theo, the boy who threatened the king by his very magical existence—no matter how little Theo wanted a throne. The throne of Fairendale can only be held by a sorcerer. No other sorcerers existed in Fairendale except for him.

Once again, Theo shoves away his thoughts.

Before he left Lincastle, Theo slipped away from the Enchantress, under the guise of collecting lunch, and located the structure where he took August and the other lost boys he helped escape from the king's men while his family ran in the other direction. August and the lost boys were not outside or inside the structure, but Theo reinforced its spell of protection, in hopes that they would return and be further shielded from the horrors he had seen in his travels.

Theo's eyes wander to the blackbirds in the cart, and now his thoughts turn to Homer, the stolen blackbird—child. Who took him? Where is he? Will they find him again? Will they be able to protect him? Why was he stolen? To spin more straw into gold?

The questions are endless.

His eyes move to the Enchantress, sleeping in the cart. She did not know which child was stolen; he could tell by the look on her face when he told her. He is not sure what worries him more: the presence of the egg or the seeming lack of care from the Enchantress.

The egg. He wedged it between two of the cages so it would not roll around when the mare, whom he has affectionately called Lightning Flower (Lightning for short), began to walk. He knows it is a dragon egg. He worries that it is a dragon egg. Dragons have never been kind to those who steal eggs. And what if it is a trap and…

No, he will not think about that.

"Good girl," Theo says, patting the mare's long neck. He guides her slightly east, straight toward the land of Fairendale. She does not resist. She has been a faithful horse and never seems to grow tired. It is particularly amazing, considering how far they have traveled. Has the magic sustained her, or is she magical herself? When he touches her, Theo can feel a certain vibration, as though there is more than mere equestrian energy moving through her. But perhaps it is merely his imagination; he always did have a large one.

Theo found Lightning in the stables outside Fairendale castle. He wonders, now, to whom she belonged. He will return her when he is finished. She deserves at least that.

Theo continues moving on, walking beside Lightning and trying not to look back at the blackbirds and the egg lodged between them. He would like to forget about the egg. He would like to forget about everything that has loose ends and fragmented connections. The looking ball, for example. Here they are, traveling back to Eastermoor, when they have already been to this land once—even battled an army of Were creatures (he does not look forward to doing that again). They will rescue another lost girl of Fairendale. They have already rescued a lost girl of Fairendale in Eastermoor; why is it that the ball did not show them both girls? And are there more?

He wonders if it would be better, more productive, to stick around the land, to ignore whatever directions the looking ball will give them after they secure this girl, to show the ball they do not like this game it is playing.

They might do well enough searching for the children on their own. But to linger in a land such as Eastermoor? With Were creatures?

The Huntsman shudders.

No, perhaps it would be better to experiment in a safer land. Is there such a land?

Theo glances back, to see if the Enchantress has woken. She has been sleeping for the better part of the afternoon. The sun is sinking low now. Will she be angry with him for not waking her? He decides to brave her wrath, if it comes. She has grown pale and sickly in the days they have been traveling. She uses too much of her magic, and the use is continuous; Theo cannot think of a single time, except when she is sleeping—and possibly even then—that she is not using some sort of magic. To speed them along, to keep them safe from creatures and other dangers, to turn children into blackbirds.

This journey will kill her. He will step in before it does.

His thoughts find their way back to Homer. What if he is only the first of the children they lose? What if every child, once found, is lost again, to some mysterious person or place? What if their quest is never done and Theo cannot turn his attention to finding his family?

He wishes he had never encountered the Bonnacon.

His nose is still recovering. And a child, formerly found, is missing.

He has reinforced the Enchantress's Protection spell around the cart and the horse and himself. The only way someone might have slipped in was if exhaustion left holes in the fabric of protection. He has tried to repair them, but he is not much stronger than the Enchantress currently. His magic is demanding much as well.

Perhaps this quest will demand everything from him and the Enchantress in the end, but they cannot give up.

A question announces itself: Is the Enchantress on his side? Perhaps it would be better to strike out on his own, to leave her lying in the woods while he takes the cart and the horse and locates the remaining lost children. But he does not have a looking ball, and, besides, he would never do such a thing; his mother and father taught him to be a better gentleman than that. He has come to care about the Enchantress during their travels together. His cheeks warm thinking about it. She reminds him of a girl he knew in the village of Fairendale. A girl he misses. A girl he would like to find.

So Theo continues on. Through thick copses, beside violet streams, past trees that grow larger and wider and more knotted as he nears Fairendale.

Into woods that darken more every day.

Calvin has brought Garth to the secret door that leads to the dungeons beneath the dungeons inside Fairendale castle. He points. "There," he says.

Garth looks at him as though he is jesting. "You must be frank with me," Garth says. "There is no door where you are pointing."

Calvin studies him for a moment, and Garth feels his certainty waver briefly. He looks back at the wall, but it is still that: a wall. There is no door. So he says, again, "There is no door."

"You cannot see it?" Calvin says. His eyes narrow, and his head tilts. "It is right there." He points more furiously, as though that will make the door appear.

Garth squints his eyes. He shakes his head. He presses his hand against the wall and traces an imaginary pattern, but he feels nothing that could be a doorway— or even a dent. The wall is perfectly smooth.

"You are touching it," Calvin says.

Garth huffs out a breath. "There is no door," he says again. He folds his arms across his chest and fixes at Calvin what he hopes is a steely gaze. This is no game. This is serious work.

"You cannot see it?" Calvin says.

"No," Garth says. "Because it is not there."

"But it is. Right there." Calvin's voice rises a bit. His cheeks turn red.

"I think something has happened to your head." Garth's anger is more than ready to meet Calvin's. He does not like being taken for a fool. And, besides that, something has been weighing on him heavily for quite a long time. He has wanted to venture down to the dungeons to see if one or more of his eleven brothers and sisters are behind bars. He has not written to his mother in much too long, and he thinks that any news he might provide about where they are would be good for her. (Garth used to return home every evening when his duties at the castle were done—but after the villagers' raid on the castle, the entire staff, excepting him, Calvin, and Cook, fled. He had felt it necessary since then to room at the castle. Besides, remaining at the castle gives him distance from his mother, who used to ask him, every day, if he had word of his brothers and sisters. No. He didn't.)

He would like to tell her that he has been busy caring for his brothers and sisters, and that is why he has not recently written. She would be delighted—relieved—to know they are alive. As would he.

But there is no door.

"I cannot believe you cannot see it," Calvin says.

"I cannot believe you see a door where none exists," Garth retorts.

"There is a door," Calvin says.

"There is not."

"Is too."

"Is not."

The two boys are acting much younger than their years; Garth turned seventeen two days ago (he did not realize it, because the castle calendars are all in disarray, so, alas, he did not even have a lovely cake to celebrate. His mother's note of birthday blessings was delivered that same day, by carrier pigeon, along with a heartfelt entreaty to come eat the cake she baked for the occasion. Garth has not recently checked the castle mail room. He will no doubt be sorry when he does; a cake does not keep forever.). Calvin is a boy of fourteen.

Calvin lets out a long breath. "I had hoped the queen was mistaken."

Garth unfolds his arms and drops them to his side. "The queen? Mistaken about what?"

"She told me that I am the only one who can see the door." Calvin stares at the wall—at the door?—and glowers. "I thought maybe younger people could see it."

"The queen could not?" Garth says.

"No."

"And you are not playing a game because you do not want anyone else discovering the entrance?"

Calvin's nostrils flare and his eyes turn flinty. "Why would I do that?"

Garth shrugs. He can find no good reason; he trusts Calvin.

Calvin moves forward, seems to turn a handle, and disappears.

"Calvin?" Garth touches the wall, but his friend is not there. It is as though Calvin were an apparition that slipped through a wall. "Calvin!"

Calvin reappears. "You see?" he says, a look of satisfaction plain across his face. "I went through the door."

Garth nods. "Yes," he says. "I see."

They are quiet for a few moments before Calvin says, "The queen says it is an enchanted door."

"There is an enchanted door in the village," Garth says. He remembers his mother talking about it. He never saw it or walked through it. His chest aches. Perhaps he is not permitted to see anything magical. Or do anything great. Or be anything other than who he is: a king's page.

"Why would someone use an enchanted door?" Calvin says. "For criminals?"

Garth considers. Why would you need a secret dungeon for those who deserved to be locked away? Would not the regular castle dungeons be sufficient enough to hold them?

Unless the prisoners had magic.

"Perhaps it is only for the magical people," Garth says.

"Or the people one locks up secretly," Calvin says. "For one's own purposes."

"Are others down there?" Garth says.

"There are bones."

"Bones?"

"Bones that glow blue," Calvin says. "With magic."

Garth does not say anything. He cannot think of anything to say. He would like to see these bones, would like to see the children, would like to know if his brothers and sisters are among them. He suspects that some are; he has eleven of them, after all. Seven brothers and four sisters.

He does not like to think of them trapped in a dark dungeon, but it is better than the alternative: fleeing the king, traveling through unknown kingdoms, and braving the dangerous woods and the creatures living in them. At least in a dungeon they are relatively safe.

"They have food enough?" Garth says, thinking out loud.

"I delivered to them bowls of everlasting soup," Calvin says. "Cook made it."

"And water?" Garth says. Garth is not surprised about Cook's magic; he and Calvin have already discussed it at length.

Calvin bites his bottom lip. "They drink from a supply that drips from the ceiling." He wrinkles his nose. "I suppose I could ask Cook to make them something better."

"And none have died?" Garth says.

Calvin is quiet for a good amount of time, during which Garth imagines his brothers and sisters lying on the cold stone floor, not breathing. His hands start to sweat. But Calvin says, "I do not think any of the children have died. But the prophets…" He lets his words trail off, and Garth guesses their meaning: either prophets have died or Calvin is not sure.

They both lapse into a thinking silence.

After some time Calvin says, "I think Cook intends to leave again." The words drop between them, heavy and unexpected.

"She only just returned," Garth says.

"She has taught me how to sustain the garden, how to chop vegetables, how to cook certain foods, especially soup." Calvin knots his hands together. "It is as though she is trying to apprentice me to her job."

"Oh," Garth says. Oh.

Well. They managed well enough without Cook before. They can do it again.

Had they managed? The castle, as he remembers, was in dire need of an orderly presence. The gardens nearly dried up, which means the food nearly disappeared, which means they might have died, if left to their own devices.

Garth will not think about that just now.

"Hello." A voice startles them from their separate thoughts. Calvin and Garth look up, but there is no one in the hall. Something scuttles across Garth's foot, and he lets loose a high-pitched shriek.

"Oh, hello," Calvin says. He greets the mouse by name—Gus—as Garth watches in horror. He must be hallucinating. He must be more tired than he thought, or perhaps he is still sleeping, trapped in a dream. He has never seen a mouse that talks.

What is this world in which mice can talk?

"Are you coming to visit the children?" says the mouse called Gus.

"I was trying to bring a…" Calvin seems to struggle with his words for a moment. He glances at Garth and looks back at Gus. "A friend."

Gus is dangerously close to Garth's foot. The mouse taps Garth's toes with his walking stick—is it a walking stick? Garth cannot be sure. What he can be sure of, however, is that he does not like mice—never has. He jerks his foot out of the mouse's reach and presses his hand to his mouth so he will not let loose another high-pitched shriek.

Garth is not discriminatory in his dislike; he has never liked *any* rodents. Even ones that walk like humans and talk like them, too.

Perhaps especially those.

Gus chuckles. "I do not think he likes me much."

Calvin narrows his eyes at Garth and says, "I think he is only surprised."

Gus nods. "I am a talking mouse," he says. "It is quite unusual."

Unusual. That is putting it mildly. Garth would have called it outlandish.

Two other mice join Gus. "Hello Timothy and Florence," Calvin says, as though he knows these white mice, too.

Garth's mouth drops open, but he has no time to say

anything before Gus says, "Only one is permitted through the door. That is you, Calvin."

"The queen told me as much," Calvin says. "I hoped she was mistaken."

"M-m-more p-p-people." Garth stops and tries again. This time he does not stammer. "More people are allowed through the secret door in Fairendale."

Gus turns his face toward Garth, but not quite.

"They are blind," Calvin mouths.

Garth nods. He supposes he would believe anything at this point.

"The doors are similar," Gus says. "But not identical. They are used for different purposes. One for meeting, one for hiding away. Or so they say."

Garth wants to ask who says, but one of the other mice walks nearer to him, and he is too busy pressing his back against the wall, willing the mouse to go away, go away, go far, far away.

"There is no need to be afraid of us," says Gus.

"None at all, Gus," says the other mouse, tall and thin where Gus is somewhat squat and fat.

"Timmy, this is Garth," Calvin says. "He is the page of the king."

All three mice turn in Garth's direction. He knows they cannot see him, but still he flinches. It has become hard to breathe; Garth would like to get out of here as quickly as possible.

"Pleased to meet you," says Gus for the three of them. "We are the blind mice of Fairendale castle, formerly of Lincastle and the Evil Queen's abode."

Garth makes a strangled noise in the back of his throat.

"They will not hurt you," Calvin says.

Garth does not answer, for fear that he will stammer again and make even more obvious his absolute terror. He flattens himself further against the wall, trying to press himself invisible. Garth once had an ugly experience with rodents, back before he was chosen as the king's page. It happened in his cottage in Fairendale village. Two of his brothers—twins—enjoyed playing with rats. Those same brothers also enjoyed practical jokes. And while Garth was sleeping soundly one night (he was a very sound sleeper, and noises did not bother him in the least, before the Rodent Nightmare, as he termed it), he awoke to find a sickening number of rats surrounding him in his bed, their beady eyes gleaming in the dark. Garth screamed and bolted from the room, out the doors, and into the village streets. His brothers found him by the cove where the sheep were watered, and they were unable to stop laughing as they dragged him back home, as if *they* were the older brothers (they were younger by almost five years).

Garth, on the other hand, was unable to forget.

"You are leaning on the door, Garth," Calvin says. Garth looks behind him, at the wall. He has backed himself into a corner.

A corner that is not the same place where Calvin originally pointed out the door. Calvin seems to guess what he is thinking; he says, "It moves."

It sounds even more preposterous now, but what is Garth supposed to think?

He says nothing in reply.

The mice move toward the door, which means they move toward Garth. He slides slightly to the right and tries to distract himself with a question. "Why are you permitted through the door if there is only one?"

The question hangs in the air. Gus tilts his head and says, simply, "We are mice, not people. If we could not go through the door, we would find other ways into the hidden dungeons." The three mice vanish through the wall, it seems. Garth looks at Calvin.

Calvin says, "I suppose I should check on them. The children, I mean. I am sorry you cannot come with me." He starts toward Garth, too, and vanishes through the wall. Garth moves as though to follow but crushes his nose against the wall. He backs up, rubbing it.

It was worth a try.

He turns away. He will not write his mother, but he will sketch the faces of his brothers and sisters. He will send Calvin with a message next time. He will find them.

He must. He is their oldest brother, their leader, their hope.

Calvin leaves Garth where he is standing, white-faced, outside the door. He glances back, but Garth has not followed him in. Did he try? Calvin wonders what it looked like on the outside—did Calvin disappear through a wall? What will Garth think?

He could tell Garth was rattled by both the appearance of the mice and the truth of the secret door. To be honest, he is rattled by the latter; he hoped that perhaps the door would let two people through it, since he and Garth were not quite grown yet. But one person is one person, he supposes.

The question, *Why*, echoes through his mind.

He asked it of the queen; she said he was chosen to care for the children. To save them.

He does not know how.

He does not know why he has been chosen.

He has never been anyone great. In fact, he has only ever been wholly undesirable; he learned that after his parents died in the land of Ashvale, where a Fire Mountain wiped out the entire population—including the only two people in the world who loved him unconditionally. He was visiting an elderly aunt and uncle here in Fairendale—an aunt and uncle who did not want him, it turns out—when the disaster happened. They fought, within his hearing, about where next to send Calvin, and while they fought, he wandered down the road to Fairendale castle, knocked on the castle doors, and asked if there were any positions available. Cook took him into her kitchen, but she did not want him, either. She merely felt sorry for him.

Cook. She will leave him soon. He can feel it, the dread creeping up into his chest.

Her former absence is proof of his ineptitude. The castle nearly fell completely apart while she was gone. She brings structure and order and hope.

Yes, mostly she brings hope.

Calvin straightens his shoulders. He sees the light ahead. He hears the voices.

"It is an ancient spell that hides the door." The voice at his feet startles him. He stops, gasping.

"We did not mean to startle you," Gus says.

"I was only making an observation," Timothy says.

Florence grunts.

Calvin looks back up the way he came, but he cannot see a door. The mice stare as though they can see it, though.

"It is very ancient," Gus says.

"Do you think the spell can be broken?" Calvin says. He has not considered this possibility until now, but did not every spell have a counter spell? He does not know enough about magic, since he was never gifted with it.

"Perhaps," Gus says. "By the right person."

"But that still leaves a locked dungeon," Calvin says. "And no key."

"Yes," Gus says. His voice softens.

Calvin did not like the mice at first, did not trust them. But the days have passed, and they have done nothing but help, and it is a comforting thing to share a burden like this one. Calvin has asked the mice if they know where lies the key to release the children from their cell inside the dungeons beneath the dungeons. They know no more than he does. And the helplessness, however disappointing it is, links them together.

When the mice first arrived, Calvin asked Yerin why they were here. Yerin could not answer that question.

And when he then asked how old these mice might be, Yerin said that, too, was impossible to tell. But he added that when all mysteries are revealed as they are (which is a mysterious thing to Calvin; he does not understand what the prophet means), questions will, at last, be answered.

When will all mysteries be revealed as they are?

It is only one of his many, many questions. Only one of the many mysteries of which he cannot make sense. Only one of the many reasons he believes that the door was wrong to choose him.

Should it not have chosen someone more capable, someone more intelligent, someone more magical, perhaps?

For a while, he even neglected to feed the prisoners here, so busy was he with his castle duties. But now the children and whatever prophets remain awake (there is only one, in fact) have a pot of soup that will never run out. They will be sustained, and tonight Calvin will ask Cook for a pitcher of fresh water, enchanted the same way. They will have no more need of his visits then.

Calvin's chest aches. Will they still want him to come? The mice give them information. What need have they of him?

Though he cannot answer that question, either, he

will still come. For the girl.

For Agnes.

She is blind. She lives in utter and total darkness, and yet the way her face glows tells Calvin that she finds joy in the smallest moments. He would like to know how to do this, too. He would like to learn from her. He would like to feel something besides this constant aching.

Calvin moves past the mice, past many iron cells. They have nothing in them except, perhaps, the bones of prisoners who died here. He does not turn to look. He does not believe these dungeons were used frequently; they smell of must and earth, not death.

The children and the prophets are kept in a cell at the end of this long hallway. It is the largest cell in the dungeons. He has heard it said that these cells are enchanted, that even sorcerers and sorceresses cannot get out. He supposes that would be a reason for kings to use these dungeons—to keep magical people from escaping.

Calvin is halfway down the hallway when Gus's voice reaches him again. "If you and your friend would like to know more about this magical door, you will have to find the Old Man's Great Book."

Yerin has mentioned this magical book a time or two; Calvin forgot all about it, consumed by his need to find the key. "Where is it?" he says.

"The prophet Aleen brought one to the castle," Gus says. "We found it in the castle library, under an enchantment."

"What kind of enchantment?" Calvin turns to the mouse now. His eyes are not used to the darkness peering back at him from this direction. He blinks a few times before he can see the three mice.

"An invisible one," Timothy says.

"To some," Gus says. "Not all."

Calvin nods. It will likely be invisible to him, then. He says, "Can you tell me exactly where you found it?"

"On a table, where the queen was sitting," Gus says.

"The magical queen," Timothy says.

Calvin shakes his head. "The queen does not have magic."

Gus gives him a strange smile. "Does she not?"

Calvin shakes his head again. Perhaps the mice are not as wise as he thought. He begins to turn away.

"We have been reading the Old Man's Great Book," Gus says.

Calvin spins back around. "How are you reading the book if you are blind?"

The mice are quiet for a moment. Then Gus says, "The book reads to us. In our minds."

Calvin shakes his head. Magic is so strange. "And

have you found the key to the cell?" he says.

Gus shakes his head. "No mention of a key," he says.

"None at all," Timothy says.

Florence shrugs.

"But we have not read the entire thing," Gus says.

"It is a very big book," Timothy says.

Florence nods.

"That is why we have not brought it to the dungeons," Gus says.

"It is much too heavy," Timothy says.

Florence grunts.

Well. Calvin will tell Garth about the Old Man's Great Book. Perhaps that is the part Garth will play in all of this, if he cannot come here to the dungeons. Garth will not be suspected roaming the halls, heading to the castle library. Calvin, on the other hand, is expected to be in the kitchen. Not that there is anyone to notice such things—except the monster-woman on Fairendale's throne (she is neither the queen nor the king; she is a usurper).

Calvin peers into the darkness, toward the magical door. Perhaps he should go now and tell Garth. He is likely still pacing in front of the door, wondering when Calvin will reemerge from the wall. (Calvin is wrong about this; Garth has gone in search of some food and is now, at this very moment, raiding the castle kitchen. Arguing and fighting off mice and searching for a door that, for him, does not exist, has made him exceptionally hungry.)

Calvin decides to visit Yerin and the children first, however. He and the mice reach the cell at the same time.

"Calvin," Yerin says.

"How are you, Yerin?" Calvin says. "Can you see?"

Yerin shakes his head, his eyes like glass. "No."

Days ago, the old prophet woke up blind.

"We found the Old Man's Great Book," Gus announces.

"It was too heavy to carry," Timothy says. "But it is here in the castle. In the library, to be more precise."

"I will try to bring it," Calvin says.

"It is Aleen's copy," Yerin says. "But perhaps it will restore my sight. Perhaps I will be able to See before…" Yerin does not finish what he is saying. The dread in Calvin's chest hangs heavier.

Yerin clears his throat. "There are only three copies of the Old Man's Great Book in the world," he says. "It is a very valuable book."

"Where are the others?" Calvin says.

Yerin shakes his head. "That I do not know," he says. "Scattered about the realm, I suppose." He is quiet for a moment before he continues. "They took it away from Aleen when they sent her to these dungeons. She told me that as soon as she lost the book, her Sight began to fail her. She thought it had something to do with the Book."

"But you do not?" Calvin says.

Yerin shakes his head. "I believe it has something to do with the end."

Agnes gasps. "No," she says, but Yerin pats her hand.

"Hush, child," he says. "We have time."

Calvin wishes he could erase the look of complete sadness that crosses Agnes's face. He says, "I will find the book. I will bring it."

Yerin nods. "I believe that will be best," he says. "To have the book here, where no one else might get it." His eyes look up, as though he is seeing through the floors of the castle.

He is thinking of the monster. What would happen if the monster found the Old Man's Great Book? Calvin is not sure he really wants to know.

"I am still looking for the key," he says, as much to distract himself as everyone else.

"Perhaps the Book will help with that, too," Yerin says. "Though I think it unwise to risk your life for this key." Calvin feels a rush of affection for the old prophet. He is still trying to talk Calvin out of searching.

"I will not give up," Calvin says.

"It is dangerous," Agnes says. Her eyes have turned toward him, though he knows she cannot see him. He would like to touch her hand, but he remains where he is.

"It is worth it," he says.

Is not freedom worth any risk?

"First, you must find the book," Yerin says. "You must make sure it is safe. You must bring it here, if you can."

"I will," Calvin says.

He has almost taken his leave when Yerin says, "The bones, Calvin?" He forgets every time he visits that Yerin likes to know the status of the bones.

A shiver skates down Calvin's back. He closes his eyes, then turns them toward the cell in which the bones lie. He can see them, regular bones arranged into the form of a person—a whole person, not half of one, as they were the last time he visited. He starts with the good news. "They are no longer glowing," he says. "But they are also no longer half a person."

"What are they, then?" Yerin says. It sounds as if he already knows.

"A complete person," Calvin says. He regrets the words immediately; the children gasp and cry out.

"Children," Yerin says. "All will be well. Do not worry."

Calvin would like to believe his words, but he sees the lines of worry that dart across the prophet's face before he smooths it into the content face of a wrinkled old man. Yerin smiles in Calvin's direction. "Thank you, Calvin," he says. "Be careful in all you do."

Calvin turns and heads toward the seemingly endless stairs that will lead him to the invisible door, where Garth is likely still waiting for him (Garth is, in actuality, now walking the castle hall aimlessly, looking for something else to do. He recently finished drawing a mustache on the faces of the first king and prince of Fairendale (King Cornelius and his son, Prince Earl), a wild crop of hair on the head of the grown-up prince (that is, King Earl, second king of Fairendale), and a pirate's eye patch over one of King Sebastien's eyes, after which he fled from the portrait hallway before someone discovered his work. He will be delighted to join Calvin in looking for the Old Man's Great Book.).

The darkness does not bother Calvin anymore, but he is still relieved to burst through the invisible wall and into the light.

# Freedom

The same evening she was visited by a strange prophet, Mira asked her maidservant to bring her the bearskin. Her maidservant knew the ritual. The girl's earthy eyes grew wide, and she hesitated for a moment. Mira knew it was because the last time Mira had used the bearskin she had nearly not woken up—she had practically become a bear. And who knew if it would happen again; perhaps Mira would meet the prophet as an eternal bear.

It was a risk she was willing to take—not only for the promise of escape but also because of what the prophet had said: She was needed to help her brother, the brother she had never even known existed. How could she help her brother locked in a tower on the Varena Isles?

She could not.

So she waved her hand and said, "Do not worry; I will wear it only for a small amount of time," and the maidservant nodded her head and hurried on her way.

At a quarter past eight, the maidservant returned with some new linens for Mira's bed. Hidden in their silken stack was the bearskin.

Mira waited until half past eleven, when her father had been in his bedchamber for an hour, before she slipped it onto her shoulders. The maidservant shoved a wheelbarrow into Mira's towered room, and as soon as Mira sank into the wheelbarrow, she arrived at the docks.

The wheelbarrow was a magical portal of sorts.

Bregdon was waiting. He greeted her with a wide smile on his face.

"You are a large bear," he said. She could hear the laughter latching his words.

Mira stood on two feet, and her shape shrunk into that of a young woman, covered by a violet cloak. It was a much smoother transition than it had been last time, and the gladness spread through her like a warm puff of air. She was free.

She was free.

Bregdon took her hand, pulled her into a small boat, and pushed them away from the docks. The water splashed along the sides of the boat, but the world was otherwise silent. Mira looked up at the stars.

She was free.

The voice of the prophet startled her when he spoke. "In the land of Fairendale, you will be a shape shifter."

Mira shuddered at the thought; shape shifters were evil creatures in the Varena Isles. She did not want to be one. "Do I have a choice?"

Bregdon gazed at her over one bony shoulder. "Do you desire magic?"

Mira answered without any hesitation: "No." Magic only led to isolation and danger.

Bregdon turned to face her fully, his lips lifting at the corners, as though he knew her every thought. And perhaps he did. He said, "That is why the magic chose you."

The words carved out a space in Mira's chest, curled up into a warm ball, and settled there. She was not sure if she wanted to be chosen by magic, either, but to simply be chosen at all—it was a lovely thought.

"In the land to which we journey, there are other shape shifters," Bregdon said. "You will be their leader."

Mira shook her head. In the Varena Isles, the shape shifters were cast off, considered both dangerous and savage, much like the land's sorcerers and sorceresses. They were feared, not understood, and, as such, they were mostly ignored. If met, they were killed.

They did not band together in communities. The people of the Varena Isles would have never allowed something so human of those they considered inhuman.

The disparity between her land and the land the prophet described is what caused Mira to say, "What do you mean, their leader?"

"I do not entirely know what it means," Bregdon said. "I only know that you will be their leader. And that you will do much good in the land."

Mira stared out at the sea, and they were quiet for a very long time. Mira dozed, then woke, then dozed again. She woke and watched the sun rise in an explosion of color, red and orange and pink meeting in both sky and sea, one line of yellow reaching all the way to their boat. Mira had never been this far from the Varena Isles. She had never felt this close to her beloved.

Her chest throbbed.

The prophet's words came again, though he had not spoken: *You will do much good in the land.*

It is all she had ever wanted to do. It is why she had not gone with her beloved, Anthony, to sail the seas. She was glad that she would be permitted to do good now, whatever that looked like—shape shifter, sorceress, woman. She had lived much too long in a cage, and it was marvelous to be free.

The sun warmed her face, a promise.

*You will do much good in the land.*

Yes. She would certainly try.

"Anthony will not return to the Varena Isles," Bregdon said after a time. "He might be able to find you in Fairendale."

"Might?" Mira said. She must have misunderstood the prophet before. He had said her beloved *would* find her, not *might.*

"Fairendale is not an easy land to find," Bregdon said. "But its magic will not last forever. A time is coming, soon, when the magic will begin to fade. I have seen it in my Visions."

Mira said nothing. The Old Man, as she had come to call him in her mind, said many strange and incomprehensible things. She did not think questions would clarify.

But the prophet continued. Perhaps he could feel the uncertainty hanging between them. "You see," he said, "the land of Fairendale, back when it was first raised from the bottom of the sea, was cloaked by an enchantment. No man would be able to find it except for the right one. And the right one did find it, and he settled in the land and brought other people to it. Some of them found Fairendale, and some of them died on the sea, searching." The prophet paused, staring out at the sea that had taken many sailors. "But though the right people came to Fairendale, they were only people. And people are not perfect."

Mira said nothing.

"Fairendale was a paradise once, before its people invited into their ranks the attractive vices of darkness. Such is humanity. It was only a matter of time." The prophet sighed. "Now there are men stealing thrones and dangerous creatures in woods and questions that do not have answers."

Mira's heart began to thump. Was the Old Man bringing her to a land torn by war and want? She had no need of that sort of life, even if it was a world of magic. Bregdon's gaze met Mira's. The yellow rimming the green in his eyes grew somewhat more pronounced. "But you and I will change that. It will take some time, but in the end..." He did not finish. He only smiled, wrinkles rippling across the pale skin of his face.

Mira could think of nothing to say except, "I did not know such a land existed."

"It is not on any modern-day maps," Bregdon said. His eyes shimmered. "Fairendale is cloaked by a Concealment spell that prevents it from being seen by sailors.”

So this was why he said Anthony might not be able to find Fairendale. The ache in her heart pulsed.

She did not realize the prophet had moved until he touched her arm. “Do not underestimate the power of love,” he said. His eyes were smiling, fixed on the sky. It had become a brilliant blue.

The prophet adjusted the one sail on the boat and turned his face to the sun. Mira watched the glittering sea, trying not to wonder about what waited beneath its depths, trying not to notice just how small this boat was.

After a time of sailing in silence, only the rustling of the sea between them, Mira said, “Why does my brother need my help?”

“Brendon,” Bregdon said. “That is your brother’s name.”

“Brendon,” Mira said. The name felt as though it had belonged to her since the beginning of time.

“He is the king of Fairendale,” Bregdon said. He stared out at the endless sea. “A very good one.”

The briny wind picked up a little, drying her tears. She had never known she was not alone in this world, though she had always felt the missing piece.

A brother.

“He is your twin,” Bregdon said. “Which is why you,

too, retain the gift of magic."

"But I was no sorceress in the Varena Isles," Mira said, and as soon as the words slipped from her mouth, she knew they were not entirely true.

Bregdon did not say anything; perhaps he, too, knew.

After a time, he said, "Your brother is the king of a desirable throne. He needs your help keeping it." He let the words sink in before he said, "Your magic will come fully alive on the soil of Fairendale." He looked at her, his eyes unreadable, mysterious, the green deeper and the yellow paler. "This is because you were made for this land."

She did not understand what Bregdon was saying, but she had lost all ability to use her voice. She turned her face to the sea and let the wind howl through the broken places inside, let it curl around the walls she had assembled so carefully, let it trace the spidering cracks and wedge into their spaces and weaken what remained.

She let it set her free.

# Revelation

It is early, early morning, before the sun has even risen, when darkness still reigns over the cottages in the village of Fairendale. Cora is already up. She intends to bring the blackbird—the prince—to the dragon. She alerted the dragon of her intention yesterday (she wanted him to wait so that he would know she is the one with the power in this relationship—if it can be called such) by blowing a message into the air (this simplistic magic, it seems, still works; she is thoroughly confused by her magic's unpredictability now, and it is not an agreeable place to be. Cora prefers control). She will keep the prince safe. She has a plan, of course.

She sneaks quietly into the secret passage beneath the fountains of Fairendale, the place where the village people, historically, met to send messages—by light—to

Prince Wendell when they needed his help. That was all before King Sebastien banished Prince Wendell and the whole world turned upside down.

Cora hardly remembers that time. It is, to her, like a dream that ended on a nightmare. She prefers not to think of it at all.

No one is in the underground room, which is not surprising. Cora crosses it and opens a small door that used to hide a pantry filled with emergency supplies. The village of Fairendale has been in such a state in recent months that the emergency supplies are not nearly as numerous as they once were, so there is space to enter and stand and even shut the door behind oneself if one would like to be alone.

Which is precisely what Cora would like to be.

Cora strikes a match and lights the single torch that hangs above the provision store. She looks around the room. There is the bird, sleeping with his head tucked under a wing. He stirs. She waits. And while she waits, she attempts a spell. Nothing happens.

She has attempted many spells over the course of the last several days, and none has worked. Her magic, mysterious in the first place for the simple fact that she retained it after birthing a magical daughter (in the land of Fairendale, magic is passed on to children, stripped from parents the moment a child is born—unless one has elected to become a prophet, which is a form of magic but does not demand a large store), has now become bound in some way. It has not disappeared; she can still feel it pulsing inside her, and she used it for the message she sent to the dragon. But her magic, it seems, cannot handle anything more complicated. It is maddening.

Cora clenches her fists but remains quiet. She tries another spell. Nothing.

Nothing, nothing, nothing. She cannot even turn the ring on the third finger of her left hand into the staff it used to be.

Now she cannot contain her anger. She growls—a feminine growl, but a growl all the same. The bird stirs and blinks its sleepy eyes. Cora glares at the bird—who is really Prince Virgil, son of Queen Clarion and King Willis. Prince Virgil was never an early riser, and he looks as though he is none too pleased at having been woken before the sun is up—not that he would be able to tell; the one window in this paltry pantry is a faux window. It looks out on earth, not a lovely landscape. This room is underground, remember, and windows do not work underground.

So Prince Virgil really has no way of knowing what time it is. Still, he blinks his beady eyes and twitters a protest.

"Time to wake," Cora says. Her voice is not gentle but somewhat harsh. She takes a breath and lets it out. No need to take out her anger on the bird—the prince. It is not his fault she cannot do magic.

It is the dragon's.

Cora holds out the first two fingers on her right hand, and, like a trained pet, the bird moves to sit on them. She carries him out to the larger room and sets him on a table. He hops to the middle. She tries her magic again. It does not work.

Cora slams her hand against the tabletop, and a sharp jab of pain makes her cry out. She turns the cry into a frustrated shriek. The bird ruffles his feathers and hops back a couple of steps.

All she wants to do is turn the boy back into a boy. All she wants to do is dismiss herself from being a dragon rider. All she wants to do is what is right for the realm.

What is right for the realm, or what is right for her?

Cora flings away the question; Sir Greyson will not make her doubt herself. Never.

She clenches her jaw and turns back to the blackbird who is a boy. She fears she is running out of time. She does not know if there has ever been a boy or a girl or a man or a woman who wore the skin of a blackbird for so long. Shape shifters, if they wear their shape shifting skin for too long, will remain in that skin forevermore. Is the same true of one who is turned into an animal by way of a magical spell?

Cora does not know. She has never had access to the literature that would answer this question. She might have, once, if she had been a princess and not merely a sorceress.

A sorceress who can no longer perform magic. It is a disappointing, vexing outcome.

It has been nearly two moons since Prince Virgil was turned into a blackbird—since she, herself, channeled the dark magic and spoke the words required for this transformation.

It is not a good sign.

Cora hunches her shoulders and presses her elbows into her knees. If she has lost the only leverage she had in the first place—her magic—then all her plans will shatter. She is supposed to be the most powerful sorceress in Fairendale. Now what is she?

Nothing more than a woman who has lost her child.

Mercy. Her plans have taken her mind off her daughter's disappearance. She needs them. She needs distraction.

The question snakes in: What if magic vanishes when

the child to whom a sorceress was supposed to gift her magic (Mercy had magic—quite a strong gift) dies?

Cora swallows hard and gives her head a vicious shake. She will not accept that. Mercy is alive. Cora's loss of magic is due to something else entirely. Cora *had* gifted her magic; she simply had not given away all of it. And still Mercy was the most powerful apprentice to magic in the village of Fairendale. Everyone knew it. Cora did nothing wrong. She did not ask to keep the magic. Yet it remained.

Cora looks around the room. She must turn the boy back into a boy before she visits the dragon. What else might work?

Only magic.

The bird twitters. Cora waves her hand and tries the spell again. She gathers him into her hands and touches his wings to her ring—her staff. She tosses him into the air and watches him soar around the room on wings she cannot wear here in this underground space—another mysterious limitation.

Perhaps the solution is to remove the prince from the room. At least then—when she is a blackbird—she might communicate with him, tell him what she is attempting to do, ask if he knows anything about magic. She suspects he was not a magical boy, though he was next in line for the throne of Fairendale. She believes that is why King Willis gave the orders to capture all the children of Fairendale—because the throne was threatened by the presence of another magical boy.

None if it has been confirmed, but Cora is wise in the ways of desperation.

Cora shoves out from behind the table, on which the blackbird sits, watching her, once more. He ruffles his feathers and tweets. Cora ignores him.

She needs her magic. She needs it to find her daughter, to return the prince to his human skin, to save the realm as she has promised.

To save those she loves.

Her plans are falling apart, but that has never stopped Cora. No, she will prevail. She always has.

She will start with finding out what happened to her magic. She eyes Prince Virgil the blackbird. Her plans for him will have to wait. The dragon will be furious, but she must do what she must do.

Cora puts Prince Virgil back in his holding cell (the pantry, she means). She looks at him for a long moment before turning away.

Magic is necessary. Her hand has been forced.

Cora stalks toward the door, turning over several of the tables on her way out.

A little message for Sir Greyson. He will know what she means.

He always did.

He waits in the shadows, barely breathing, inside the room beneath the Fairendale fountains.

He has been here for some time. Cora did not notice him pressed up against the earthy wall. She did not even look his way, must not have felt his presence, ignored his eyes burning into her back. Perhaps their connection has severed more completely than he thought.

He has seen everything.

He watched Cora attempt to turn the blackbird back into a boy. He watched her fail. He watched her storm from the room, with a bit of a limp—from a dragon wound—and turn over tables as she went.

He knows what it means. He does not like it. What does she plan to do? He wishes he knew.

Sir Greyson has returned to the village, because the king has returned to the throne room of Fairendale castle, where a cursed throne and a mysterious mirror wield their evil influence, along with a monster. He does not know for sure that the king has reverted to his old, cursed self, but Sir Greyson has seen the monster. He does not think this monster will have much trouble turning King Willis's heart again. He thought his plan to save the king and queen by ferreting them from the castle and hiding them elsewhere might work, but now the queen wants to remain with the king and make sure that all is well. In a matter of moments, his plan to save the royal family disintegrated.

He learned this through a note sent by the queen; she said, "Do not bother coming, Sir Greyson."

Queen Clarion has charged Sir Greyson with protecting her son—at any cost—and bringing him back to the castle when the kingdom has been set aright. And when will that be? It is impossible to know—impossible to guess, even.

Prince Virgil, a blackbird. Is allowing the continuation of this transformation protecting the prince? Especially now that it appears Cora cannot turn him back into a boy? Sir Greyson rubs his hand over his mouth.

Protect the prince, or protect the woman he, Sir Greyson, loved?

Loves.

Sir Greyson rubs his chest.

It is all too complicated.

When he is sure Cora is not returning to this room, he emerges from the shadows. He rights some of the tables, pushes in the chairs, looks toward the door where the blackbird is kept. He stands there for a moment, looking around the room. He wonders if Cora thought about the ears that might be listening and the eyes that might be watching. She is growing careless, and he knows what that means, too. She is desperate.

A dragon rider. Sir Greyson swallows hard and dives toward the entrance, which spits him out on the hill leading down from the fountains (one never really knows where the secret door will eject its visitor). He tucks and rolls his way down, landing, as always, on his feet. He walks toward his mother's cottage.

His mother will know what to do. She always does.

She is stretched out on her bed. She has been in bed for many days now. He has brought her more medicine, but he does not think it will help much here at the end.

The end. What will he do without his mother? He can hardly breathe for the ache.

She is not sleeping; she is reading. He does not feel badly about interrupting. "Hello, Mother," he says as he sits by her side.

His mother puts down the book and saves its place with her leg. "Hello, Grey," she says. Her voice sounds younger than it has in the past. His heart hopes. "I thought you had business at the castle."

Sir Greyson's stomach twists. "Yes, I did," he says, looking down at his hands. He tries to think of something to say, but his mind is an endless blank. Too much has happened. Too much has disappointed.

"And how is our king?" His mother takes Sir Greyson's hand.

"Well, there is a monster on the throne." The words spill out.

His mother stares at him, but she does not seem surprised. She only says, "It is unlike you to call names like that, Grey," as though she is chastising him, as though he is a little boy. Her lips have a hard line to them, and her eyes flash. It has been some time since he has seen this much life in her. All it took was mentioning a monster.

Sir Greyson smiles a shaking smile. "There is someone who has come to Fairendale. Someone who now sits on the throne."

"Another king?" His mother tries to sit up more, but she falls back onto her pillows in a coughing fit.

"Do not exert yourself too much, Mother," Sir Greyson says.

She shakes her head and holds up one finger. He

waits. When she is finished with the coughing, she says, "What do you mean someone has come? Has another foolish boy attempted to steal the throne?"

"No," Sir Greyson says. "This is a…" He hesitates, unsure what to call her. "A woman?" It comes out like a question.

His mother tilts her head. "Is she a woman or something else?"

"I am not entirely sure," Sir Greyson says. "Part woman, part monster, I think. Part living, part dead."

His mother frowns and gazes toward a wall, as though she is thinking. At last she says, "A Black Eyed Being, you mean?"

Sir Greyson shakes his head. "Not as far as I know. She looks…" She is difficult to describe. Sir Greyson searches his mind for adequate words. "She is something entirely different. Perhaps enchanted with magic and brought back to life."

"Oh," his mother says. She appears somewhat worried. Does she know something she is not telling him?

"Mother?" he says.

She waves a hand. "It is nothing."

He waits for a moment, but she does not continue. So he says, "I did not come to talk to you about this."

His mother's eyes study his face. "Something else is

bothering you," she says. "Is it…?"

"Cora," he says.

"Ah," his mother says. She smiles a knowing smile. "Love."

Sir Greyson's cheeks burst into flame. He clears his throat. Where to start?

He starts at the beginning. He tells her everything he has seen and all they have said and what he heard.

When he is finished, his mother says, "Poor Cora. Poor, dear child."

Sir Greyson feels a spot of annoyance begin to bloom in his chest. Cora is not a child, and she is not poor and helpless. She is a powerful sorceress.

Or she was.

His mother seems to intuit that he is annoyed. She says, "Cora, I fear, is in over her head. She is confused. She needs wise counsel. She needs trust. She needs love."

Sir Greyson swallows the protest that is building in his throat. He knows his mother is a wise woman. He knows it is in his best interest to listen.

"She has not had an easy life," his mother continues, and that is the breaking point for Sir Greyson.

Because who among us has had an easy life?

He says, "How do you know she did not have an easy life? She had a mother and a father. Her mother died, yes, but her father loved her well enough."

His mother fixes her eyes on him. "There are things besides family that can break us, my dear," she says, after which she settles into such a violent coughing spell that Sir Greyson feels alarm. He pats his mother's arm and threads his fingers through her hand. He wills her to be well, but he knows it is not enough.

He needs her for so much.

"Cora has been here," his mother says into the quiet.

Sir Greyson's breath catches in his throat. "What?" he says.

His mother nods. "Did you not know that she looks in on me while you are away?"

Sir Greyson shakes his head.

His mother closes her eyes. "Well, she does. She always has." Her voice is papery thin.

Sir Greyson sits with this information for several minutes. His chest swells at the thought of Cora caring for his mother. So she does love someone, at least.

"She loves you," his mother says. He stares at her face, but she does not open her eyes. A warmth crawls toward his belly.

He clears his throat.

"I do not know if I should leave the king with the monster," he says. "I tried to get him out of the castle, and he agreed to come with me, to give up his throne, to be a king who fled a kingdom."

"And what happened?" His mother is still awake. He was not sure.

"The monster," Sir Greyson says. "And the throne."

"The throne," his mother says.

"The curse," Sir Greyson adds.

"And you have left him in the castle now."

"Yes."

"In the throne room, with the cursed throne?"

"And the monster." Sir Greyson can already feel the regret closing off the back of his throat. He should not have left the castle.

But what about his mother?

His mother is quiet for a time. And when she speaks again, it is only to say this: "I am sure you will do what is in your heart. What is best."

But he needs her to tell him what to do. He needs her to say what is best. He does not know; can she not see that?

What if he makes the wrong decision—as he did with his men in the dragon lands—and he costs more people their lives? What if he has to carry that for the rest of his life? Does he not already carry enough?

His mother's voice breaks into his thoughts. It is so

soft he can almost imagine what he hears. "You are the son of a king, after all."

The words lift his eyes to her face. Her eyes are glassy, unfocused. Is she dreaming with her eyes open? Has she just called him the son of a king?

"What?" Sir Greyson says. But his mother's eyes flutter, and she drifts off to sleep, her breathing deepening and widening and filling all the space between them. He stifles the urge to shake her awake, to demand an answer, to hear the truth.

But he knows she was likely caught in a delirious dream, the kind one has before falling asleep.

He pulls the medicine from his pocket, and as his mother sleeps, he administers the proper dose by needle into her left arm. It is pocked with needle marks. Necessary but distressing.

He watches his mother sleep for a time, turning over his thoughts, considering plans.

It is, as it has always been, a choice between love and love. Love for a mother and love for a king. He does not add Cora to the equation; it would make it too complicated.

And as Sir Greyson sits, the choice becomes clearer and clearer.

He will return to the castle. He will save the king. He

will conquer the monster.

He is no hero, but he will certainly try.

Sir Greyson kisses his mother's forehead, rises, and turns toward the door. Before he leaves the cottage, he scribbles some words on a piece of scrap parchment, lets it fall to the desk in the corner. It is written to no one in particular. It is merely words, arranged in strange couples.

A message for Cora. She will know what it means.

She always did.

Rose has wasted too much time thinking about all she has lost; even she knows this. She has been unable to rouse herself to get a splash of water to drink or a bite to eat (fortunately, her back rests against the trunk of a tree that is the favorite spot of an endless supply of red ants; she has been collecting them all day and using her magic to create a chocolate coating so they go down a bit easier). She is feeling both exhausted and restless. Is she anxious to move on? She cannot tell.

Her mind is a muddle. Her confidence is consumed. Her senses are off-kilter. She cannot trust what she sees or hears or smells or tastes or touches. She hardly knows what she is doing in these strange, dark woods, can hardly remember her own name.

Rose. That is her name. She is supposed to look like a rose. It is why her mother and father named her after a flower.

She does not look like a rose now. And so begins the inventory of her losses, once again.

Midway through her despondent day, a girl crosses Rose's path—the same one she saw—was it yesterday? Days ago? She cannot recall how much time has passed.

It is not so surprising to see this lovely girl with hair the color of cherrywood. Of course the universe would deign to show Rose more obviously all that she has lost.

But what does surprise Rose is that this girl is being stalked by a very large black wolf.

Does she always come with a wild animal?

Rose sits up. The girl must be saved. Rose must be the one to save her. And she is about to call out, distract the wolf from the girl, when a movement in the opposite direction commands her attention. A snake is watching her.

A snake! Rose has never, ever, ever liked snakes—not when Niram brought them home and called them "non-venomous," not when her best friend Aurora turned one into a floppy hat and wore it an entire autumn, not when her father set the meat on their table and said it was as good as any other meat and stop complaining.

Rose finds that she cannot move—is it despondency or terror? It makes no matter; the fact is she cannot move, not even a little. And so the snake draws closer, and as it draws closer, it lifts its body into the air, as though it is walking upright. Rose blinks, and the snake flickers into a beautiful woman with long black hair and flashing green eyes. Rose blinks a second time, and it is a snake again, still upright, its neck curved and ready to strike.

She must be dreaming.

The creature moves slowly, deliberately, as though it has come just for her. It flickers into a woman and back into a snake again. Three more times it does this shifting of shapes, and Rose is still paralyzed. She would like to move—run, to be more precise—but her limbs do not cooperate.

"Help!" she would like to say, but she also cannot speak. Rose closes her eyes. So the end will come like this. After all this time. After all she has survived, she will be taken by a nagini.

She knows about naginis, because her mother kept on their bookshelves a book about the dangerous creatures of the forests. Rose never read the book, though her curiosity about other subjects was untamable. She did not like frightful things and preferred to pretend they did not exist (except in her stories). But Niram loved this particular book; he would study it and tell her all about the fearsome creatures, regardless of whether or not she wanted to hear (to reiterate: she did not). Before coming to these woods, Rose never believed such creatures existed, but the things she has seen...well. Perhaps someone will find her bark books and know that Rose did, at least, exist once upon a time.

In the split seconds before the nagini reaches her, Rose files through the random bits of information in her brain. She remembers Niram telling her about a princess who was guarded by a nagini, though the creatures typically dwelled in lakes and underground streams and guarded magical gems and precious stones. Guarding a princess was an unusual deviation for a creature more concerned with the purity of water and the conservation of the natural environment. She must have been a lovely princess to attract the notice of a nagini.

Rose is so lost in her own thoughts that she startles when a low voice says, "What are you doing here?" She opens her eyes. The nagini has returned to her woman form. Rose can almost convince herself that the creature in front of her is nothing more than a woman, except that the nagini's forked tongue makes an appearance. And something about the eyes, green and reptilian, a thin spear of black carving out their middle.

Rose tries to speak, but she is too terrified. She only stares at the smooth brown skin and the large eyes and thinks about how she would have liked to Vanish and reappear as a nagini. She would be a snake, yes, but her woman form would, at least, be better than her current bent and broken form.

The nagini waits for a moment, but when Rose offers no words, she says, "You are disturbing the natural order of things." Her voice has a distinctive hissing quality about it. She draws closer to Rose. Rose tries to scramble back, but her limbs, still, are not obeying. The woman is so close to Rose that either could reach out and touch the other.

A snap sounds, and Rose is released from whatever held her. She is, at last, in full possession of her limbs and her mind. She reaches toward the stud in her nose, but nothing happens. She presses it again. This time it is her staff that does not cooperate.

Something is terribly wrong.

Rose yelps and turns around, fully intending to run, but the nagini moves faster than she can. It wraps around her in a flash. She is being crushed by it, the snake's triangular head hovers in her face, she is staring at those awful green eyes, she is—

But the girl who wandered through the clearing is suddenly there with a sword or a dagger or some other sharp weapon that slices through the nagini's tail. The nagini shrinks into a regular-sized snake and retreats into the grass, slithering away so quickly neither girl can follow. For a moment, Rose stands staring at the young and lovely girl with the cherrywood hair.

Then she runs.

She does not even say thank you (her mother would tell her that manners are as important as beauty). She is consumed by one thought: *I am a monster.*

To the girl with the shining hair and midnight-sky eyes and perfect skin, she will certainly look like a monster. Rose's skin is carved with wrinkles and pitted with the holes that come from ancient living.

The girl, however, chases after Rose, calling, "I see you! There is no use trying to get away."

Rose stumbles behind a fortuitously hollow tree and scrambles into the backside hole, which is perfectly cut for her. She tries to still her breath while peering out of another, smaller, frontside hole. She presses her feet as far back as she can manage, hoping they are lost in shadows.

The girl moves from tree to tree. "The woods are

dangerous," she says as she moves. "The naginis are not the only creatures you will meet. Especially the closer we get to a full moon."

Rose shivers, but she does not emerge.

Another girl skips into the clearing, this one with white hair and large blue eyes and the palest skin one could ever imagine. She is a stark contrast to the golden brown girl beside her. "Red, it is time for you to come home," the fair girl says.

"I only need a moment more, White," the dark girl says. "I am looking for something."

"What are you playing now?" White says, and she smiles, as though she expects something like this from Red. But Red continues moving from tree to tree.

Rose watches her, pressing herself flatter against the inside of the tree. She reminds herself she must not be seen; to be seen is to be feared in her current state. Her addled mind does not for a moment think about how she was already seen, and she was not feared.

Red sighs. "I suppose I will have to look tomorrow."

White nods. "Mother is ready for supper."

"I saw a nagini," Red tells the other girl. "Perhaps that means there is a treasure of some kind that will change our futures."

"You are always dreaming grand dreams," White

says. She flips her hair over her shoulder. "There is no way to change our destinies. It has been written for us already."

"You do not believe me," Red says.

White looks at the ground. "There are no naginis in these woods, Red."

"How do you know?" Red puts her hands on her hips. Rose almost smiles.

"I simply do," White says, turning toward the way she came. "Come."

"Someone else was here, too," Red says. "She had a lovely dress. I did not get a good look at her face, but I think she might be a sorceress."

Relief crests in Rose's chest. Red did not see her face. Rose will keep it that way. No sense in giving the girl nightmares.

And yet, the ache in her chest widens. To be seen is sometimes the greatest gift of all.

The girls' voices reach Rose, even though she can no longer see them.

"You always did have fanciful stories." White, most likely.

"They are not stories. They are truth." Red.

The large black wolf Rose saw before follows the two girls. Why do so many creatures follow Red?

Their voices fade, until Rose is completely and utterly alone again. She looks around her with a new kind of terror. She does not think she is strong or brave enough to survive these dangerous woods.

She huddles in the hollow of the tree and tries to forget all about who she has become—but who could ever do that?

Though it is high noon, Theo shivers. He and the Enchantress have reached the land of Fairendale, and the air here is chilly—much chillier than he remembers it being the last time he was here or, for that matter, at any time in his life. He skirted them around the entire village, so as not to be seen by the king, which could lead to questions they cannot answer. So he is on the north side of the Weeping Woods, but even the north side was never so cold.

So dark, too. Theo peers into the trees. He can see nothing, and sunset is still half a day away, by his estimation.

He straightens. He has a strange feeling about these woods. "Something is tracking us," he says. Something sinister, he thinks, but he chooses not to say this aloud.

"Have no worries," the Enchantress says. "Nothing can breach my wall."

Theo is not so sure. It is true that he was never a huntsman before calling himself one (the Enchantress does not know this), but even he can tell that whatever is tracking him—creature, undead, the Grim Reaper, perhaps—will not be held off with a Protection spell.

And, besides, something has already slipped through the spell.

He glances at the Enchantress out of the corner of his eye. He is surprised she does not feel it as well, the sickening sense of dread.

"You think I am not strong enough to protect us?" The Enchantress does not look at him when she asks the question.

Theo waits a long moment before he says, "I think you spend too much of your magic. And what happens if it weakens?"

"Magic does not weaken," the Enchantress says.

"But sorcerers do." He is careful not to say *sorceresses.* He believes the Enchantress might take offense at the insinuation that magical females weaken. And he would be correct.

The Enchantress opens her mouth to say something but closes it again. Theo can tell that she is thinking and that her thoughts trail the same line his do. She wonders, too.

"They were protected, were they not?" he says.

The Enchantress shakes her head and raises her eyes to the sky, what little of it they can see through the tops of the trees. It is the same color as slate.

He wonders if the sun shone at all in the days they were gone.

Theo has almost forgotten his question when the Enchantress says, "They were protected with the same spell I have used all along. I reinforced it after the child was stolen." She cuts her eyes at him and drops them to her hands. "No one should have been able to breach the Protection spell I cast. I do not know how it happened."

He has mulled it over in the silence of his travels. The Enchantress slept the entire time, so he did not have anything to distract him from the mulling. He does not look at her when he says, "Do you feel weaker?"

The Enchantress lets loose a short laugh, but it does not sound amused. "You think I would tell you—"

"It is for our safety," he says. He presses his lips together so he will not say what is foremost in his mind: *I can help.*

He does help in whatever ways he can, in ways she cannot see, where cracks have begun to appear. But he fears that there will be more cracks the longer they travel. He will use more and more of his magic, which means he, too, will grow weaker. And what then?

The Enchantress takes such a long time to answer that Theo thinks she does not intend to. So it surprises him when she says, "I feel weak all the time. I do what I can."

"No one is saying you are not doing everything you can," Theo says. His heart urges him to tell her that he can share the burden of what magic demands. But his head seals his mouth shut. He swallows the words. He cannot be sure of her reaction; it might change everything.

The dread grows. He is afraid he is doing all of this wrong. He wishes he could talk to his father. Theo winds his fingers together and clears his throat. "It is so quiet."

"It is high noon," the Enchantress says. "The people are sleeping."

Theo looks up at her. "How do you know they are sleeping?"

The Enchantress does not meet his eyes, but he notices that her cheeks turn pink, and so does her throat. A tell.

She shrugs with one shoulder. "Perhaps I have spied on the people of Fairendale a time or two."

Theo smiles, in spite of himself. "I prefer to call it observing."

The Enchantress gives him a strange look. Theo's heart thumps. He once had this very exchange in the streets of Fairendale, with Mercy. She caught him spying —observing, rather—on the butcher, to see which of his sister's sheep would be slaughtered that day. He saw the butcher slaughter a sheep that was not part of Hazel's flock, and he smiled and wondered aloud from where this replacement sheep came. Mercy caught him in mid-wonder.

Theo feels heat gather in his own cheeks and throat now. He stares at the ground. The air crackles between them. He knows, in the way the presence of all complicated secrets are known, that the Enchantress is keeping something from him. Something important that she elects not to tell him—because she does not trust him? Because she does not feel the same connection with him that he feels with her? Because she plans to be done with this quest and leave for good?

In his moment of gloom, he conveniently forgets that he, too, is keeping something very important from the Enchantress.

Theo decides to change the subject, steer their conversation back to more solid ground. Words walk out before he can stop them. "What happens when your magic takes everything from you?"

Well, so much for solid ground.

The Enchantress frowns at him. There is a long silence before she says, "Why do you think it will take everything?"

Has she not noticed how thin and pale she has become?

"Because magic always has a price," Theo says, and it is as though the dread were waiting for these very words. It burrows in and balloons.

"Perhaps most magic does," the Enchantress says. Her lips quiver. He notices.

"You do not think your magic takes anything from you?" Theo says.

The Enchantress does not answer.

"If you have a looking glass," Theo says, but he does not finish. He has a looking glass in his magical pack. He has practically everything one could need for a journey, except food. He could not figure out how to preserve it without magic.

He reaches into the pack, but the Enchantress holds up her hand. "I do not wish to see," she says. "I do what I must."

"But it will take everything." His words are soft,

almost a whisper. "And when it takes everything, what will we do?"

The Enchantress presses her lips together. Her eyes look older, wearied by the travel and the magic she expends every moment of every day. "I do what I must."

"Let me help."

Theo is as surprised by the words as the Enchantress is. Her eyes grow wide. But when she laughs, Theo unwinds by degrees. She does not believe him. Perhaps it is better.

She says, "And how could you, a huntsman, help me, an Enchantress?" She turns her eyes to him. They glisten.

"With magic," he says. He meets her gaze.

Surely she has known. Surely she could sense it. But he sees the shock slide over her features—eyebrows rise, eyes widen more, mouth slackens. "You are a huntsman."

He has gone too far to turn back now. So he says, "A huntsman with magic." Theo feels the Enchantress's gaze burning over his face, but he keeps his eyes locked on the ground. He wills her to understand why he kept this secret.

This secret. He has protected it for so long. It has cost him everything—his mother, his father, his twin sister. And now he has told an Enchantress. He has no idea what she will do with this information.

"A huntsman with magic." The Enchantress's voice is a whisper, but it is wide with wonder, as though pieces are falling into place. Theo almost lifts his eyes to hers, but he is not willing to give up the second part of his secret yet.

The silence is long and thick. In it, Theo thinks about his family, particularly his sister. He wishes he could ask the Enchantress for a look in the looking ball, for a glimpse of Hazel. He saw a flicker of her one night; she was lying in a grassy clearing, her eyes closed. He has tested his magic, however. He still possesses the gift. The rules of magic say that if one magical twin dies and the other remains living, the living one loses his or her magical powers.

So she cannot be dead, can she?

He does not know. Nothing feels assured anymore. He does not understand the rules of magic. Sometimes it seems as though there are no rules. If his father were here, Theo would ask him many, many questions. Arthur always had an explanation for everything—one he and the other magical children taught by Arthur could understand. And if Arthur was not around to answer questions, Theo would ask Hazel and Mercy.

How he misses them all.

Theo glances at the Enchantress but looks away when he sees that her eyes are still fixed on him.

"What would you do with your magic?" she says into the large and jagged space between them. He can hear a tinge of suspicion in her voice.

"I would help you protect our journey," Theo says. As he has already done. He keeps this bit to himself. He will help in greater proportion, if she agrees. She can expend less energy, and he can use more.

The Enchantress does not say anything for some time. At last, she says, "It could be a good solution. Temporarily."

It is the first time she has admitted that he might be integral to this quest. He knows that she has thought it before, but there is a large difference between thinking and speaking aloud. Speaking aloud makes something real.

He is necessary. His magic will be needed. He has waited to use it, without hiding, for a very long time.

The Enchantress and Theo remain as they are, both staring into the forest, both thinking their own thoughts that likely contain both relief and a growing ball of dread.

# Home

Their journey was smooth sailing, for the most part. Mira assumed that Bregdon was using his magic to help propel them along their way, and she had no complaints about that. She was not nearly as suspicious of magic as she was terrified of the sea, and, besides, she had always been a rebel. Though the people in her land regarded magic as malevolent and evil, Mira had never ascribed to their puritanical ways. Anthony had been an evil demon to them as well, and she knew better than that.

She questioned everything they believed, but she had been alone in her questions.

What would the people think if they knew her father, their king, had relied on magic to attempt to save his queen?

"We must take care up ahead," Bregdon said into the

stillness of midday. Mira heard a distant sound, a melody of the strangest tone and quality.

"The sirens," Mira said. Anthony had told her about them; he had lost many men to the sirens.

"They are dangerous to man and woman," Bregdon said, as though, once again, he could hear her thoughts. "Both fall for their song and their beauty."

Mira could hear the song now, could feel it snaking into her chest. It was a song she recognized, a song she knew, a song of life and love lost. She leaned forward.

"No!" The prophet's voice was loud in her ear.

"But they are singing the song he sang." Her voice was small and childlike.

It was true; the melody caught on the air was a song of the sea, the same one Anthony would sing to her on the nights they sat on the docks, watching the water. She could even hear his voice echoing across the sea, joining with the other voices. Was Anthony there, among the sirens? Had he been waiting on the sea cliffs all this time? Is that why she had been so eager to leave the Varena Isles, because she somehow knew she would see him again, if only she took to the sea?

She had to know. She steered the wheel toward the rocks lining the horizon.

"No!" Bregdon pulled against her, and they struggled

for a moment. The prophet was old, but he was stronger than he looked, and he wrestled the wheel away from her with one forceful yank.

The rocks sped toward them, much faster than they should have with only the water and the wind helping them. It was love, Mira thought, drawing them into its cove. Mira could feel the song pooling in her chest, latching on, tugging harder, more insistently.

"We must go!" she said. "He is there, on the rocks!" Her throat ached. The words burned. Her hands shook. She wrenched the wheel again.

"Mira!" Bregdon wrenched it back. Mira stumbled.

"But he is there!" She could taste the salty tears on her cheeks.

"He is not!" the prophet said. He could not steer the wheel and tend to the sail, and the wind was swatting them closer to the rocks. "Help, Mira. We will not survive if you do not help." Mira closed her eyes.

"I must find him!" she said.

"He is not there!" Bregdon said. The wind screamed. "Seal your ears, and you will know!" His eyes had become green, a glowing green, a green that seeped into her bones and lifted her hands to her ears.

Seal your ears. Seal your ears. Seal your ears.

She could still hear them, could still hear *him*, and she

lunged for the wheel again. The prophet was ready. As soon as he touched her, all sound melted from the world.

The prophet's eyes were wide, watching her. He had done this. He had stolen her hearing. But she could think again, and when she lifted her eyes to the rocks, she saw them, the sirens, waiting. Their eyes were cat-like, some glowing yellow, some forest green, some cerulean. They were beautiful faces, but as she passed them, they smiled, and their teeth were made of nightmares.

A green glow surrounded their boat and remained until they were safely past the rocks.

Mira's breath came in gasps. It was some minutes—perhaps even hours; time was fluid on the ocean—before her hearing returned to her. She hung her head and whispered, "I am sorry." And then, "Thank you."

The prophet must be more than a prophet, more than a magical man. He must be other-worldly to have resisted that beautiful song. Mira wondered what the sirens sang for him.

Bregdon turned to face Mira. "Those who have never heard the sirens are the most vulnerable to their song," he said. "I have had much practice." A fleeting expression of pain crossed his face.

She dared not ask about it. Instead, she said, "You have left your land often?"

"Here and there." Bregdon's eyes met hers. He looked exceptionally tired. He must have spent much magic saving them from the rocks. Mira looked at the ground.

"Perhaps it would do you good to rest a bit," she said. She tried not to think about how she was the cause of his exhaustion.

"We are nearly there," Bregdon said.

Surprise lifted Mira to her feet. She gazed at the horizon but could see no land. "You must have sped us along," Mira said. She had not expected a journey so short. She felt both relieved and despondent to leave the rocking of the sea.

Bregdon did not say anything for a time. He let the wind whisper and moan. But, at last, he said, "Fairendale is a long way from your land, but we made good time."

Mira searched the horizon but still saw nothing. She thought about what the prophet had said. Fairendale was far from the Varena Isles, and it was invisible. Did Anthony have a chance of finding her? Perhaps it was a mistake to come with the prophet. Perhaps love would not be strong enough to bring him to her. How could it? She had been so easily swayed by sirens. What would happen to a man at sea, hungry for land? Would he even venture this far?

Perhaps her magic could draw him to the land. Mira knew nothing of magic, had no training of any kind, and she could not even guess what might be in store for her with the possession of stronger magic. She looked at her hands, folded them in her lap, and then unfolded them to stare at their lines and edges again.

The only thing she knew of magic was that sorcerers needed a staff. She had never had a staff.

The unrest grew louder the longer they sailed in silence.

Mira kept her eyes on the horizon. A heavy mist cloaked the way ahead, and Mira looked at the prophet. He seemed unconcerned, so she tried to calm her overzealous heart. Mists in the land of the Varena Isles meant magic, and not the good kind.

But Bregdon did not turn aside. In fact, he sailed right through the mist.

On the other side of it was a land of the loveliest green.

"There it is," Bregdon said.

"Oh," Mira said. And what was contained in that one word were many other words: *I have never seen a land so lovely as this.*

Bregdon beamed at her, then turned his attention back to the land. "It is cloaked by a powerful spell, a partition of sorts," he said. "The one who began this spell was a powerful sorceress."

"Still living?" she said.

"No," Bregdon said. "But another continues it." He gave Mira a significant look that she did not understand. "She is a tree."

And then Mira knew. Her mother was here on this land, too.

Mira was home.

# Resolution

Rose wakes with a hunger unlike anything she has ever felt. The chocolate-covered ants were not substantial enough. When she stands, she feels faint, as though she might topple over at the smallest gust of wind. She will have to do something about her food situation. She cannot subsist solely on insects for much longer.

The sun has already climbed high in the sky when she emerges from her hollowed-out tree. She walks in no particular direction, having learned, by now, that freshwater tributaries spider all through the woods, and if she walks long enough, she will find one. She does not bother keeping away from the tributaries now; she has seen enough of these woods to know she will never be safe, completely. She merely hopes the tributary she finds will have no fearsome creatures living in it. She hopes, instead, there will be fish. She has never filleted a fish, but perhaps she might try.

She finds a tributary in little time. She examines it, sees nothing of concern, and so bends and drinks straight from the pool. It teems with fish.

Perhaps her fortune is changing.

She has just straightened up, just summoned her staff (which works fine now, after the danger of the nagini is gone) and prepared to spear a fish when a grunt spins her around. In front of her is a large wild boar, his beady eyes glaring at her. He has a dark bristly coat, a ridge of hair along his spine and gleaming cream tusks.

If she were not in this predicament, Rose might laugh at her appalling fortune. It seems her luck has not changed at all.

But at least she has her staff.

Unfortunately, the staff does nothing, and the world slips off-kilter again.

She is going to die.

The options flash through her mind: She could run, but if she runs, the boar would easily catch her; she knows wild boars are fast. She has watched them running through this very forest and marveled at their speed. She would never be able to outrun this one, not even with magic. Not even if her staff were working.

Rose glares at her staff.

She could face the boar, but she has nothing with which to fight him. He, on the other hand, has a face full of tusks, and all it would take is one well-placed blow to make her bleed.

Rose shakes her head at her lack of viable options.

But it does not matter what her options are; it turns out that her fortune has not yet embraced the "ill" side completely. Red crashes into the clearing, her hair a mess around her face.

"There you are," she says. Rose blinks and holds a finger up to her lips. She moves her hands out in front of her, as though telling the young girl to remain still, as though that would help at all. It is too late. Not only has Red spied the boar, but the boar has spied Red.

For the flash of a moment, Rose thinks about running. The boar has other prey now, and the only person she would need to outrun is Red. She has always been good at running.

And then she remembers, once again, that she is an old woman.

Curse these creaking bones.

Rose remains where she is.

This time half her face is turned toward Red. She hopes it is the better half.

The boar does not immediately attack them, and Red does not immediately attack the boar, and in the moment or so of indecision, Rose decides to act on her original plan: Run.

This she does. Red's voice twirls on the wind. "Do not be afraid," she says. "I will protect you."

The boar does not follow, and Rose does not stop.

It is good for the girl to learn how reprehensible Rose is. She is not a friend. She is not a pet. She is nothing but an old, selfish woman who would leave a child to die.

Rose nearly runs into the large black wolf she saw following Red yesterday. The wolf bares his teeth, and Rose runs in another direction, her feet already aching, her chest already burning, her legs already liquid fire. What was she thinking? Of course she could not run.

But still she does. She runs and runs and runs. She will run to the village (though she does not know if this is the right way). She will hope the creatures she left behind are not allowed in the village streets.

But what will she do in the village? How will she, a girl with no money, no jewels, no benefit of any kind, find a place to sleep? Will the people even let her in?

Her courage fails her, and Rose dives behind a tree, wincing as her hip hits the ground.

*Please leave me alone. Please leave me alone. Please leave me alone.*

She closes her eyes, but it does not stop the turning of fortune and fate.

The boar has found her, once again. But this time he stands on two cloven feet. He grunts. He moves much faster than Rose might have thought. Before she can even react, he has her hair in his fist.

His fist? But wild boars do not have fists. Rose cannot believe her eyes. They are playing tricks on her.

The boar drags her by her hair. She tries to scramble to her feet, but she trips and falls, and with each movement—scramble, trip, or fall—she feels the painful pinch in her hip. She notices an arrow lodged in the side of the boar. He appears stronger than ever.

In a haze, Rose watches Red race toward the boar and loose another arrow. Rose flinches. It will hit her, it will hit her, it will hit her. But the arrow flies straight over her head and into the belly of the boar. The boar groans but does not let go of Rose's hair.

Red releases three more arrows, and three more arrows meet the belly of the boar. Still he does not let go. Red races toward Rose, unsheathing her sword. Rose closes her eyes, preparing for the end, but, instead, she feels a release.

Her hair. Red cut her hair. Rose watches the girl cut a

line of red into the back of the boar. The boar flees, screaming, into the woods.

Red sheathes her sword and turns to Rose. "You seem to attract dangerous creatures," she says, and Rose cannot argue, though it was not always so. Red stares toward the direction in which the boar fled.

"That boar is a troublesome creature," Red continues. "It has damaged lands around Eastermoor and stolen fresh fruit from the village gardens. I think the people will be glad to see it destroyed."

Rose does not remind Red that the boar was not destroyed, that it, in fact, moved as though the arrows did not even touch it.

But she does not want to call attention to herself. So she says nothing.

"I am very sorry about your hair," Red says. She looks at Rose for the first time since speaking. And she gasps, a look of horror climbing across her face.

Rose feels the sting of that look, and it is what sets her on her aching feet and moves her legs again.

"Wait!" Red calls, but Rose does not stop, not even when Red says, "Perhaps you need a safe place to stay."

Rose runs far away from kindness and beauty and everything she cannot be.

Alfie, the youngest of what used to be the seven sons of the king of Eastermoor but is now six (a spell turned the second oldest son into a beast), is combing the woods. He is trying to recover his memory, looking for anything that appears familiar, searching for signs that what he thinks happened did, in fact, happen. Though his memory left him for a time, it has returned in patches. But they are fantastical patches: a beast, a magical girl disguised as an old crone, Were creatures turned against them all.

The memories have a dreamlike quality about them, which makes them easy to dismiss.

Except that Alfie has a small tear in his heart, where he thinks—he knows it is ridiculous—another brother might have been. Six sons of King Luca and Queen Mia. Were there not seven? And, if so, where is the missing one?

Alfie shakes his head. He has searched these woods for days—perhaps even weeks, though it is impossible to tell. The days passed in Eastermoor are long and fluid; children are permitted free and easy lives, with no set mealtimes or nap times. They are free in every sense of the word.

Sometimes that freedom gets a little out of hand. Children disappear. Tales are added to the already abundant folklore of Were creatures. The people carry on.

To tell the truth, Alfie and his royal parents and brothers, along with all the people of Eastermoor, have been under a Forgetting spell, administered when the Enchantress and the Huntsman tracked down Anna, a magical girl who reappeared, by way of the Vanishing spell, in the woods of Eastermoor, as an old crone. Anna accidentally turned Alfie's brother into a beast, and a beast he will remain until love releases him from the spell.

Alfie knows nothing of this, though he did; the Forgetting spell accomplished what it intended, though the Enchantress did not intend for his memory to recover, as it appears to be doing, if only in patches.

He remembers, vaguely, creating a house for Anna. And this lucky day, he stumbles upon it. He stands in the clearing, staring at the house that was built in the middle of the woods, and the thin tendrils of recognition creep over him. He has seen this house before; where?

Alfie stands there for a very long time. But his memory remains only patches. He cannot see the face of the woman. He knows there was a woman. She was old, but she was a child. Or so someone said. He is so confused.

No one is home.

He walks on, until a roar rumbles through the woods. Perhaps it is the beast he has seen in glimpses during his wanderings. Alfie shivers. He has never seen a creature quite like this beast, and he does not fancy meeting it. He gazes up at the sky; it is still light enough. He does not know if tonight is a full moon, but he does not want to risk getting caught here in the woods and meeting those Were creatures that populate his dreams.

What happened to his memory? Alfie attempts explanations—he fell and hit his head, he succumbed to the effects of fever, he repressed the difficult ones for self-preservation—but none of them make sense in light of what he knows of himself. He has never been afraid of memory.

So the only explanation that makes sense at all is magic.

The people of Eastermoor do not believe much in magic; they look on it with suspicion and not a little fear. It is unnatural, and they are a culture in which natural is exalted. Mostly, they pretend it does not exist. But Alfie has seen it. He has encountered it. He cannot remember who or what or where, but he remembers magic.

Alfie walks aimlessly, without a destination in sight.

He walks right past the brand new (yet decidedly ancient) castle, erected by Mira when she took pity on the beast, Alfie's missing brother, and gifted him this drafty palace so he could hide his beastly form until his story was finished and he returned (hopefully) to his princely form. The castle is hidden by a wall of brambles, which are not so unusual in the Were Woods. If Alfie were walking on the other side of them, he would likely be able to see clearly the tall spires, but because nothing alerted him to the presence of the castle behind the thick cover of brambles, he walks past with hardly a second glance.

The missing piece in him, however, he cannot shake. He knows that he is missing something, that there is something important left undone, that there is a person— maybe more than one—who has been, if not forgotten, overlooked.

The village seems to sense it, too. People have been arguing more vehemently, more readily. King Luca is petitioned many times a day, where before the people were content to settle their own disputes, which were few and far between. Arguments, too, were unnatural.

Alfie sits down on a log to think about it. He thinks about the missing place at their table, which no one mentions or seems to find unusual. He thinks about the empty bedroom in the castle and how every time he walks past it he can hear the sound of another brother's voice. He thinks about the princely crown he found in one of the storage rooms, no cobwebs curtaining its jewels, as though it were discarded moments ago.

None of it makes sense.

But is there sense to be made? Alfie is not certain of this, either.

A roar sounds again, this one more distant but also more painful. It is the cry of desolation, and Alfie finds that he must blink and wipe away tears, though he cannot explain or understand why.

He gives the sky one more long look, as though he will find answers there, and then he turns back toward the village.

It is later in the morning than it usually is when the Graces comb through all the lands, looking for upsets or holes or places of darkness that might need delicate intervention. They have already done this once today. But after morning tea, Good Cheer rose and headed toward the looking ball again, as though she had forgotten they already performed this ritual.

She flicks through the lands quickly, more than once,

like she is skipping pages in a book to find one particular passage she remembers.

"Wait. Stop," Mirth says. She points. The scene clears. Her finger rests on a spot of darkness. And when her sisters see it, too, their alarm is practically tangible, another large presence in this small room. Their knees buckle, but they hold to each other.

"What is that?" Splendor says.

Good Cheer leans in closer to the looking ball. Her face embraces the green tint of the ball so she looks like a creature from another world. The looking ball shimmers slightly, losing the scene and finding it again. It is a tree. A sickly-looking tree.

"That is The Great Tree of Helomoth," Good Cheer says, and she begins to weave a story around them.

In his travels, explorer Dale Enderling, founder of the Fairendale lands, discovered a strange tree in the Whispering Woods of Rosehaven. He named it the Great Tree of Helomoth. He stood before the tree, and this was the name upon his lips. His hand opened his journal, and this is the name it wrote, of its own accord, as though the tree had been named at the very beginning of time.

The Great Tree of Helomoth, he wrote, is larger even than the Sequecas, which are common trees in the Wishing Woods. He said it must take fifty or more men to circle its trunk with their arms. Its branches grow up and out and back down again, in what he termed a "resplendent arch." (Here, the sisters tilt their heads. The tree in front of them does not have a "resplendent arch." It appears to be weeping.)

Those who step inside the tree's glittering fold are lost momentarily to those who remain outside. The wise Dale Enderling tested this by stepping into the fold and turning around. He found himself fully encapsulated within the tree's protective cover.

He also saw a golden light glowing at the base of the tree, right where trunk meets ground.

He did not know what this glow might be, but folklore has solved the mystery. What Dale Enderling did not know at the time of discovery, and what many still do not know, is that the Great Tree of Helomoth is the tree that keeps alive all the magic in the realm of Fairendale. It maintains the balance of good and evil. It keeps Death on Death's side and Life on Life's side.

Splendor and Mirth stare at Good Cheer. They wonder, briefly, how she knows all this but they did not.

But then Good Cheer says, "The tree is dying," and they forget all about their question.

The Graces pull closer to the looking ball. This would be cause for intervention, Mirth believes. Splendor believes it, too. Good Cheer is, predictably, not so sure.

"It must be a mistake," she says. She waves her hand so the looking ball goes dark. She calls it back to life and flips through the lands until she reaches Rosehaven. The tree, fortunately, is still there, but, unfortunately, it is still dying.

Splendor and Mirth look at one another. "It is not a mistake," Mirth says. "The tree is dying. You can see how it droops and does not glitter as it once did."

Good Cheer nods, but instead of feeling better, Mirth and Splendor feel worse. Dread fills the backs of their throats in a thickening sludge. They are one and the same in this moment.

Splendor tries to clear the sludge away. "What was it the bear told us about the spinning wheel?" Splendor says, after they all stare at the tree for some minutes without talking. "Did she not mention the Great Tree of Helomoth?" As she remembers, Splendor wonders why she did not ask about this tree at the time. Perhaps there were more important things to do and know. Perhaps she had grown too accustomed to the strange names of strange wonders; she will have to remedy that, reawaken her curiosity.

Mirth snaps her finger. "They buried it beneath the tree."

"It must be removed," Good Cheer says.

"They must dig it up," Splendor says.

"And bring it here," Mirth finishes.

They pause, still gazing on the tree.

"If this tree dies…" Good Cheer's voice catches in her throat. She lifts her chin and says, "If this tree dies, the balance of good and evil, life and death will be destroyed." Her eyes tell her sisters just how worried she is about this possibility.

"Forever?" Mirth says.

Good Cheer only shakes her head, and they all think about the implications of this.

After a short time, Good Cheer says, "I can think of only one other time that this happened. The Old Man told me a story about it. The Grim Reaper was responsible then, too."

"You think this is his work?" Splendor says.

"Perhaps," Good Cheer says, and her eyes turn cloudy, hazy.

"But the bears, the shape shifters, they buried the spinning wheel here," Mirth says. "The Grim Reaper has not been near it."

Good Cheer is far away from them, lost in a vision. Her sisters wait. They are accustomed to this kind of thing, though it has not happened in some time. In fact, they are glad Good Cheer seems to have lost touch with reality; it means they will do something, at last.

Her voice, when it spills out of her, is low and hoarse. It sounds like and unlike her at the same time. "The Great Tree of Helomoth contains an eye that, when opened, will set everything right."

Mirth and Splendor look at one another again. An eye? On a tree?

"No one has ever seen this eye," Good Cheer says, in the same low and steely voice. "I have seen it."

The looking ball flashes. Mirth and Splendor peer into it, but they do not see an eye.

Mirth shrugs with one shoulder. Her eyebrows draw low over her eyes. She looks as though she is concerned for Good Cheer's state of mind. Graces are not supposed to know the future—but is this the future? Will an eye arrive, or is it already there?

She squints at the looking ball.

Good Cheer fades somewhat.

"Good Cheer?" Splendor says. She reaches out to grab Good Cheer's arm. Good Cheer solidifies but says nothing. She fades again, and this time Mirth grabs her other arm. Good Cheer faces them.

"We must summon the shape shifters," Good Cheer says. Had she noticed her fading? Splendor and Mirth do not know and do not ask. They merely give each other a glance full of all sorts of wonderings.

"Why the shape shifters?" Mirth says. "Why can we not do the work ourselves?"

"The Grim Reaper is sure to know about this soon," Good Cheer says. "And he will be there, waiting for us, when our strength is the smallest." The three Graces give a collective shiver. "This tree is significant, you see? He will know about its weakening, even if he is not responsible. He will be waiting."

The certainty with which she delivers these words erases all argument.

"We will need the shape shifters for this work," Good Cheer says. "They are the only ones who can see us and our urgency. They are the only ones the Grim Reaper cannot yet touch." Her sisters nod.

A slight aside here, if I am permitted: It is unknown why the shape shifters are the only ones, in the realm of the living, who can see the three Graces. Perhaps it is because they live such long lives. Some of the prophets, like Bregdon (who was not entirely in the realm of the living, since he died and lived again in a cyclical fashion), can see them if they have lived very long lives as well, and, of course, the undead can see them. Marion, or the Evil Queen, can see them as well, since she was invited into their circle once and refused. But to everyone else, the Graces are invisible. One can only feel their occasional influence in a life.

"So we will summon them," Good Cheer says. "And we will wait to do our greater work. It is almost time."

Once again, her sisters nod.

It is almost time.

# Disappointment

Mira and Bregdon docked in a land called Lincastle. Mira marveled at the houses that all looked like miniature castles; they were charming, and she would have liked to stay and observe more—the birds in abundance, the silver bell on the edge of the village, the castle in its domed and exotic beauty—but the prophet sped them along, hardly looking over his shoulder. When she asked him about the land, he only said, "It appears to be substantial from the outside, but it does not contain much on the inside, except, perhaps, on its perimeters." She had more questions, but he held up a hand. "There is no time. We must get to Fairendale."

Bregdon transported them to some blazing woods. Searing heat blasted at Mira's neck and throat. She had to take a step back.

"I believe we may be too late," Bregdon said, and he took Mira's hand and ran—much faster than should have been possible for a man of his age. He kept his staff raised above their heads, some sort of spell creating a sphere around them as they dashed through the torched trees and fire that could not touch them.

Mira tried not to look at the fallen dragons, but it was impossible. Her heart grew heavy, and her feet slowed.

This was a land torn apart. Why had she come?

Bregdon stopped abruptly, his arm colliding with Mira's chest. He hung his head. "We are too late," he said. The grief wrapped around his words and wormed into Mira. Her breath tangled.

"Too late for what?" She was surprised that she could speak. Her voice was high, hysterical almost.

Bregdon held a finger to his lips and pulled her behind a very large tree, around which he peered. Mira joined him. She saw a man standing some ways in front of them, on what looked like a castle lawn. A few people surrounded him. Was he her brother? He looked much too young to be her brother. And then she saw all the bodies lying around the boy in the middle. She saw the one that wore a crown. The boy bent and picked up that crown and set it on his own muddy-haired head.

"No," Mira breathed. She nearly rushed forward, but

Bregdon's grip was strong.

"Wait," he said.

She did not want to wait. She did not understand this directive. Had he not brought her here to save her brother? She pulled against Bregdon's hand. He must have used magic to hold her in place. She tried to find her own magic, the one he said would awaken when she stepped onto this land, but there was nothing.

And the anger of it all—the man who must be her brother, slain; the leaving of her homeland—for what?; the boy who would dare wear a crown that was not his to wear—slammed into her. She opened her mouth to speak, but the prophet beat her to it. "Do you feel the magic?" he said.

Mira shook her head. She did not know what magic felt like, but she knew she did not feel it.

It had been a mistake to come all this way.

"Wait here," the prophet said. He fluttered the hand that did not hold his staff. He whispered some words and stepped away from her. He bent to touch something on the edge of the clearing, but Mira could not see what it was. She watched him walk past the people who circled the boy with the crown, as though none of them could see him, and she knew that he had made himself invisible. He bent to touch one of the slain figures, and she knew the body belonged to her brother. She tried to step out from behind the tree, but her feet were stuck to the forest floor. She tried to cry out, but when she opened her mouth, she could not find her voice.

The boy with the crown strode up the stairs of the castle and through the doors. The people looked around at one another, their faces stained with dirt and blood and tears. They moved toward a dirt road, their backs bent and burdened.

Only the prophet remained. The prophet and the bodies. Mira stared at the bodies. And as she stared, the bodies disappeared. She blinked her eyes. Where had they gone? Into the ground?

Bregdon was back by her side. "We were too late," Bregdon said. "But I have tried to remedy some of it, at least."

"Why did I come here?" The words shook out of Mira, splintered and sharp.

"Never underestimate the power of love," Bregdon said. She had stumbled. He was holding her, whispering into her hair.

She wept.

They remained that way for a long while. At last, Bregdon said, "Come." He held out his hand, and Mira, not knowing what else to do, not knowing who else she could trust in this new land she had never even known existed, took it. He drew her deeper into the woods, to a house that was built long before this day. The woods were burning, but the house was not.

"Magic," Bregdon said. He stood in the doorway, and Mira knew, without asking, that he was not going to come inside. He was going to leave her alone. His eyes were soft when he said, "Now I must hasten to another land."

"Take me with you." She had not meant for her voice to sound so desperate. She was a strong woman. But she did not want to be caged again.

"Here," Bregdon said. He dropped into her hands a stone, white and smooth, with a green patch on one of the sides. It was perfectly round, like no other stone she had ever seen.

"You will need this in the coming days," he said. His green eyes almost glowed as they shone into hers.

"For what?" she said.

"It is a magical stone. It will awaken your powers and tell you all you need to know." Bregdon wrapped her hand around the stone. "And you can Summon me when you need to. Though I would advise you to wait until I come to you. It is the safest way."

There were so many questions, but the one that barreled past her lips was: "But what will I do?"

"The stone will tell you all you need to know," Bregdon said again. He was already crossing the porch of the cottage, stepping down stairs into the burning woods.

"But will I see you again?" Mira said.

Bregdon waved a hand behind him. "I am as close as the stone."

Mira held the stone in her hands, rubbed it between her two palms and heard his voice, twisting on the air, rising and falling as though reading from a text. Teaching her about magic.

Mira found a rocking chair on the porch and sat down to listen.

When she finished her learning, after many days or weeks or perhaps even months had passed, Mira sewed the rock into a pocket inside her dress, where it pressed its warmth against her hip.

A cage would not hold her now.

# Risk

Cook—Mira, as we will call her from here on out—is feeling nostalgic today. She is lost in a memory of sailing the Violet Sea with the prophet Bregdon, on their way to the land of Fairendale. How is it she still remembers so much? Perhaps it is because the prophet mentioned Anthony. What had the prophet said? That Anthony would return to her? That love always finds a way?

She cannot remember; the words have grown blurry in her mind. Many years have passed. Anthony did not return. Love did not find a way, it seems.

Mira straightens her shoulders. Perhaps Anthony did not come because Mira needs to do something great. A woman does not need a man to be great. But could she not have done something great and loved, too? Could she not have been a wife and perhaps a mother and still been called to greatness?

The thoughts plague her today. Mira tries to shove them out of the way, but they are persistent things, crawling back in when she is stirring soup, descending on her shoulders when she is picking fresh tomatoes from the vine, sliding into her throat when she would sing instead. She has been silent all day, thinking of Anthony.

Thinking, too, of Calvin.

But mostly Anthony.

The prophet told her she would see Anthony again. How long will it take? Is he even still alive? If he sails the Violet Sea, does he sail toward Fairendale? Does he know she is here?

She thinks of her father. What happened after she left? Is her father still alive? She doubts that. She brought the castle to the land of Eastermoor, did she not? It was abandoned.

The thoughts culminate into a cloud of despondency. She came here to save her brother, and she did not even manage that. Perhaps that was the requirement for reuniting with her beloved, and because she missed it, they also missed their chance to live happily ever after (Mira and Anthony had long debated the term "happily ever after" when they were younger; neither was convinced such a thing existed. They knew they were in for hard work and dedication, as any marriage demands).

Mira slices fresh carrots with a good bit of violence, concentrating her anger into the cutting. She will cook another stew tonight, in the pot with the spell protecting the king's heart. She will once again protect this castle, and she will once again give most of her life to the cause.

The cause that is what? Good over evil? She could have done that in the Varena Isles. Why did Bregdon bring her here?

She has waited eighty-three years for a promise of returned love, here in the realm of Fairendale (that does not include the nearly forty years she waited in her homeland, the Varena Isles). How long must one wait?

She is tired, all out of patience, losing hope. Mira stares at her hands for a moment. Through it all she never lost hope. Will she give up, here at the end?

Is this the end?

She tries her best to shake off her gloomy thoughts and stares out the window, squinting her eyes at the woods. What she would like to see there is Bregdon walking out. It has been many years since she saw the old prophet. Perhaps he finally lived his last life. Her thoughts catch, then, on what it must have been like to live so many lives. Bregdon, at some point in their acquaintance, told Mira about his gift. He could perform his One Last

Great Act as many times as he wished; he would die and he would rise again, forever frozen in his one hundred forty-third year. Or so he thought. But perhaps forever had ended at last.

And what of the banished prince? Mira had not heard what happened to Prince Wendell after he left the kingdom of Fairendale, but she did not think he had vanished entirely. For a while King Willis, when he was a prince, looked for his brother, planned a trip around the realm to seek him. She knows this because back then she spent a good deal of time in the castle library, and she saw him there often, though he did not see her. He heard the occasional fluttering of pages, perhaps, but she kept her invisibility flawless other than that.

Mira dices some celery.

She really thought she would be someone different by now, at this age. She thought, once upon a time, that she would be Mira, powerful sorceress and wife of Anthony, living in the village of Fairendale or one of the others in the realm. There were several from which to choose; Anthony would likely have enjoyed Eastermoor, a place with few rules and Were creatures.

But she is still Cook. And Anthony is still absent.

Mira throws some of the celery into the broth, along with the stewing carrots, and tries not to notice the way some of it splashes out in drops on the iron stove. She will not clean it up.

Yes, she will. She cannot abide spots on her stove. She wipes it with a rag, nearly burning her hand in the process.

She turns away from the stew. She will let it boil for a time, as the thoughts inside her have boiled for the last hour. And she will go for a walk, try to calm her agitation.

As she walks through the hall toward the castle doors, a whisper reaches her. She looks around, but there is no one. She continues on her way, but the whisper soon snakes into her ear again. She stops and looks around, but no one is there. She stares at the wall.

Is a whisper coming from the wall?

Mira presses her hand to it and leans her ear against it. She hears the whisper, but she cannot make out what it says. No matter what she tries to do, no matter the magic she calls into her hands, no matter the wishing she presses into the wall, the whisper grows no louder. But there. She can hear something more substantial now.

Her name. It is calling her name.

Her name? Or someone else's? Now it sounds like the king's name.

Mira stands back and folds her arms across her chest.

Well. She will have to work a stronger spell into the broth tonight. She hopes the king is playing his part, because the war has only just begun.

She will get rid of that throne as soon as she can. The mirror, too.

The whisper curls into the air again. Mira shakes her head. This castle. It is cursed. Perhaps she should leave it for good. Her brother is no longer its king, after all. Why does she stay?

The face of Calvin burns into her mind, and her chest gives a wrenching twist. She rubs it.

Oh, yes.

She stays for Calvin.

For the boy she must protect.

For the son she never had.

She has remained for Calvin since he got here eight years ago. And she will continue to remain until the world is set back on its feet.

If ever it is.

Marion, who is known as the Evil Queen by both the Graces and most all of the prophets of the realm (who are, as it happens, locked away in the secret dungeons beneath the dungeons of Fairendale castle; it is unclear whether they are living or dead), has been brooding of late. Not much good comes when Marion has been brooding.

She has always done well enough on her own; in fact, working alone is what she preferred back when the prophet Bregdon rescued her from the hand of the Grim Reaper and invited her to be a Grace. She told him so. She did not become a Grace. She became, to reiterate, the Evil Queen.

But she is growing tired of not having a magical looking ball or a magical mirror (she made a magical mirror once, but she delivered it to Fairendale castle, in hopes of saving a few lives; she does not know if she succeeded, because she has no other magical mirror or a looking ball). So she is in the dark, so to speak. She does not know what happens outside of her day-to-day experience. She has witnessed the Graces gathered around their own ball, and though she has attempted to see what they see, peering through a window while they are bent over the ball, she has not succeeded. The ball merely glows green for her; there are no pictures at all.

Marion, more than anything, would like to know what is happening, would like to know where she is needed, would like to know her purpose. The prophet left her here and never returned. Why?

She could, perhaps, launch an effort to steal back the magical mirror. But she has not set foot in Fairendale castle since she was queen. And that was many, many years ago. How would it feel to walk through those halls? And does she really want to know? After all, her husband, the Good King Brendon, was no longer king. And her daughter?

What happened to her daughter, Maren?

This, of all the wonderings, is the one that haunts her most.

Marion swallows hard and tries to think about something else—anything else. She sent her eyes to the castle: the three blind mice were the closest thing Marion had to a magical looking ball or the gift of prophetic Sight, and now they, too, are in Fairendale.

Yet another reason for her to go? Perhaps.

She has nothing on which to lean anymore. And while that may be as it should be, Marion does not like being left in the dark.

The Graces have a looking ball. They can see all across the realm. They know what is happening in every corner of every kingdom.

Perhaps she will steal it.

A smile spreads across Marion's face.

The evening after Cora attempted to perform her spell on a blackbird and turn him back into a boy, Cora goes to visit the one woman in the village of Fairendale who has always been able to answer her questions in the clearest and most direct manner: Sir Greyson's mother.

Cora lost her mother when she was very young, and for a time, Cora entertained the notion that she and Sir Greyson might become more than mere friends. During this time, Sir Greyson's mother took her in, so to speak, and Cora accepted the gesture with joy. She needed a surrogate mother and the wisdom one could provide.

She still does.

When Sir Greyson was taken away by king's guard duties, Cora named herself his mother's caregiver in his absence. And, in fact, it was Sir Greyson's mother who talked Cora out of hating Sir Greyson for leaving. She talked Cora out of hating Sir Greyson for attempting to capture the children of Fairendale, too. And for trying to cross the dragon lands and nearly dying in the attempt. And for returning to the castle and the king.

The only reason Cora does not hate Sir Greyson at all is because of his wonderful mother.

Cora brushes her hands against her thighs and raises a fist to knock on the door. She knows Sir Greyson is no longer here; she watched him walk down the road to the castle herself. She tried to summon all the anger inside her, but she only felt cold. Lonely. Forlorn.

She lifts her head and pushes in through the door.

"Hello, my dear," Sir Greyson's mother says when Cora closes the door behind her. Her bed is in the great room into which the front door opens, so it is easy for her to see visitors. "You have missed Grey. He returned to the castle."

Cora's heart trips for a moment on that familiar name, but she squares her shoulders and walks farther into the room. She sits on the same chair that held Sir Greyson, and she takes his mother's hand as he likely did before he walked out of the room, out of the cottage, and out of the village.

Did he think of her when he left? She shoves the wondering away.

"Do you need anything, Bree?" Cora says. Her voice is soft and gentle, though she feels anything but calm, sitting in this house where Sir Greyson sat most recently.

Why did he not say goodbye? In spite of everything, he always said goodbye, in some way or another.

"Are you hungry?" Cora tries to distract herself with

caregiving.

To tell the truth, Cora feels even more on edge here than she did in the secret underground room and in the streets of the village and in her own empty home. There are too many memories in this house. Too many plans that did not come to pass.

Too much love here.

It is nearly suffocating.

And yet, perhaps it is the best place for her to be.

The warmth of Bree's hand spreads up Cora's arm, and Cora looks at her arm as though there is magic coursing through it. And perhaps there is.

"I am not hungry," Bree says. "I ate what Grey left me. But thank you for asking, my dear." She squeezes Cora's hand, and Cora feels the grip squeezing her heart, too.

"Would you like me to stoke the fire?" Cora gazes toward the fire, but it is already stoked. There is not really anything for her to do, then. There is no reason for her to be here. She had counted on a reason.

Bree does not say anything, but she smiles a soft sort of smile, as though she is patiently waiting for the real reason Cora came. Cora sighs. Bree could always see right through her. She should have known.

"I have misplaced my magic." Cora delivers the

declaration calmly, with an almost apologetic smile, as though she is not a wild tempest inside.

"You still have your magic," Bree says. "You have not misplaced it at all."

Bree is the only one of the villagers who knew that Cora, upon becoming a mother, still retained her gift of magic. In fact, it was Bree who assured Cora that Mercy, too, had the gift of magic and that sometimes magic chose to remain within a sorcerer or sorceress. Cora, Bree declared once upon a time, had done nothing wrong.

"Then where is it?" Cora says. "Why can I not perform spells?" Her voice has dropped to a whisper. She knows they are alone here in this cottage, but still. One never knows if there are listening ears.

If only she had been so cautious yesterday, when Sir Greyson hid in shadows and heard her long monologues spoken aloud and with passionate and angry conviction; she did not know she needed to be, though. She still does not know about his eavesdropping. And this is for the best.

Bree says, "Tell me what happened, Cora."

Cora does not know how much she should tell and how much Bree already knows. What has Sir Greyson told her? What does Sir Greyson know?

She begins with, "One day I could perform magic,

and the next day I could not."

Bree looks at her as though she knows that Cora is not telling the whole story. Cora sighs again. Why is it she always feels like a young girl in Bree's presence?

But sometimes it is good to feel like a young girl, like someone has your best interests at heart—even if it is an old woman who is the mother of the man you loved once.

Love still.

Cora rubs her chest.

She may as well get it over with. She says, "I became a dragon rider. And the next day I could perform no magic."

Bree struggles to sit up in her bed. "You became what?" Her voice sounds alarmed, but her eyes give her away. Somehow, she already knew.

Still, Cora repeats the words: "I became a dragon rider. I did not intend it. It happened."

Bree is silent for some time, long enough for Cora to squeeze in a question. "But I should not lose my magic, should I?"

In truth Cora does not know much about dragon riders. It is quite possible that riders do lose their magic, even if the dragon told her otherwise. He is a young dragon; he likely does not know everything, either. What did he say? He never wanted to have a rider? When you do not want to be something, do you know much about it at all?

"Magic is unpredictable," Bree says at last. "It is impossible to say."

"But have you ever read or heard of a rider losing her magic because of a dragon?" Cora is aware that her voice has risen slightly. She swallows and breathes.

Bree shakes her head. "No. I cannot say I have."

"Then what could it be?"

Bree shakes her head again, but she does not answer. "You know," she says, after a long silence during which Cora considers leaving and then decides to stay. She stays for this: the wisdom that she knows is about to come tumbling forth from Bree's mouth as it always does. "There are people who can help restore magic to the worthy."

"Who?" Cora says, and then: "Where?"

"They are called Mages. They live in the far north." Bree reaches out to pat Cora's hand. "But it is a very dangerous journey. No one who has attempted it has ever returned."

"I have a dragon," Cora says.

Bree smiles and shakes her head. "It is not protection enough. You would be foolish to risk it."

Cora smiles, but she does not feel it anywhere but her stiff lips. "I have always been called foolish in my life, and it has served me well, I think."

"Cora." Bree's voice is quiet but firm.

"Bree." Cora's voice is quiet but insistent. "I must."

Bree lets out a long, rattling breath that ends in a long, rattling cough. When she is finished she says, "People tell you that you cannot do something, and you do it anyway."

Cora smiles at the old woman, her heart warming with tenderness. "It is my way," she says.

Bree nods. Silence swells between them until Bree fills it with, "My son loves you very much."

Cora sucks in a breath. She looks at their hands, twisted around one another—one wrinkled and spotted, one still young enough.

It takes her a long time to speak, and when she does, she says, "I know." Her voice weighs more than the sky outside this house. She feels the words bend her shoulders.

She does know that Sir Greyson loves her. The problem has always been that he loves the king more than he loves her.

Does it matter? The question curves around her.

"I know you love him, too." Bree's voice reaches into

her mind and settles there, though Bree has not even opened her mouth to speak.

Cora gasps. "You have magic," she says. Bree does not answer; she has fallen back on her pillows and closed her eyes. The tiniest hint of a smile touches the corners of her mouth.

Cora stares at Bree for a very long time, waiting for the older woman to open her eyes, waiting for her to deny or confirm what Cora has said, but Bree's breathing deepens, as though she has fallen asleep. Cora bends to kiss her forehead, and when she turns away, it is with a genuine smile for the first time in days.

Magic, in the most unexpected of places.

And now she will go in search of reawakening her own gift. With the dragon.

Cora stands in the village, the wind whipping her hair out behind her, like a serrated flame, and eyes the woods in the direction of the dragon lands of Morad. Her chest burns. She turns away.

She cannot leave without saying goodbye.

In her own way.

King Sebastien has been missing from the mirror for

some days, and today Yasmin is, once again, trying to summon him.

She does not know how this works; she has never encountered a magic mirror, and even if she had, she has no magic remaining in her living-dead body, as she has taken to calling it (she was dead, she knows, and then she was raised to life by a scientist or a prophet or something of the sort; the details are fuzzy). Days ago she had a magical quill feather pen, but she lost it in the woods somewhere (or, rather, someone took it), and she has been unable to locate it, as have her creatures.

Yasmin is the queen of monstrous creatures. She has not been endowed with this royal title, but she knows it. She feels it.

At least she thinks she does. Sometimes she wonders if she has been led astray by some evil force. She is, after all, the Grim Reaper's minion—no, she is more than a minion; she has her mind and her will. She has plans! Is the Grim Reaper evil? Or a natural way of life? All men and women die, after all. The Grim Reaper is merely the one who collects them.

Yasmin turns toward the mirror. "Sebastien," she says. "I have need of you." He seems to be the sort of man who needs to be needed. Her son.

She had not seen him in many years, had not ever

witnessed him grown. Her heart aches. Would he have grown to become the man he became if she had lived instead of died?

These kinds of thoughts have been plaguing her lately. She has tried, unsuccessfully, to ignore them, but they always return.

"Sebastien," she calls again in her low, grainy voice. Something flickers in the mirror, and then nothing. Is it working? Should she continue trying?

Yasmin walks around the mirror, trying to find an entry point. What if she stepped into the mirror? Is such a thing possible? She finds nothing. She glances toward the throne room door—the rear one, not the double ones that open out into the long hallway connecting to the entrance of the castle. She left the king of Fairendale in the dining hall, eating his soup. On her first day here, she discovered that she could taste none of the succulent food prepared by Cook. The smells torture her, so she hides away here, while the king eats his fill.

It gives her a good reason to examine this mirror, without the king watching her from the throne, where she makes him sit night and day. The throne has some kind of enchantment on it. She thinks it will help her cause (though she has been questioning even this), which is why she makes the king sit.

Sebastien told her, days ago, about the throne's curse (he called it "advantageous"). He said this—ordering King Willis to sit on the throne—was the only way to ensure that King Willis will play on her side (and what is her side? She still is not entirely sure). And even though she is her own ruler, she thinks it wise to consider others' opinions, use them to inform her own.

Sebastien. Her son. Every time the word crosses her consciousness, she feels it like a dagger to the chest. How does a mother forsake her son? How does a mother refuse him freedom?

Yasmin gives her head a violent shake.

"Sebastien!" This time her call is a sharpened point.

A scratching sounds at the doorway. "Is something wrong, my lady?" The boy in the doorway does not look at her, and Yasmin nearly laughs to give him a good scare. But it gets caught in her throat.

This boy. What is it about this boy?

Her son.

No. She must strike the word from her mind. She almost does.

Yasmin shakes her head. "Thank you…er…" She does not know the boy's name. "I am just fine. Has the king finished his supper?"

"Almost," the boy replies, still without looking at her.

"Please send him in when he is done," she says.

"Yes, my lady," he says.

She waits until he disappears from the doorway—and several minutes after—before she turns back to the mirror, her glare fixed on her reflection. She is not so scary, is she? She is still a woman, though she has blue-tinted skin. Her eyes are still hers. She touches her right cheek, where a gash was corrected with black threads. She still needs to find a Healer, but she does not know where to start. The village of Fairendale is not as vibrant as it once was.

Yasmin folds her arms across her chest and squints at the looking glass. When she calls Sebastien, she expects him to come. She will tell him this as soon as he decides to make an appearance. They will discuss a new arrangement; if he expects her to follow through with her end of the bargain, he must follow through with his.

She has been too soft on him. And anger makes her brave.

"Sebastien." She tries one more time, but there is nothing.

Well, perhaps she will find answers in the castle library. Perhaps she will discover a way to force his hand. To summon him with success.

Yasmin lowers herself into the throne and drops her

chin to one hand. She fixes her eyes on the mirror.

And as she stares, the mirror flashes and a form appears. But it is not the form she is expecting; it is a man, but it is not Sebastien. This man is taller, thinner, like a stretched pole. He has blue eyes entirely unlike Sebastien's nearly black ones; they are paler, wider, framed by golden lashes. The figure disappears, and Yasmin squints at the mirror. The figure returns, and this time he looks at her and mouths one word: "Help."

Yasmin stands, terror crashing over her, stealing her breath, freezing her hands and legs. She tries to say something, but no words come. The mirror is empty once more.

Did she imagine what she saw? Yasmin cannot be sure. And because she cannot be sure, she tosses the red velvet curtain that is perfectly mirror-shaped over the magic mirror. She does not want to see what it has to show her, not until Sebastien returns.

She stands staring at the red curtain for a moment. And then, with swift steps, she walks out the throne room doors and into the hallway.

She goes in search of Queen Clarion this time—for female company or for another, more sinister purpose?

Yasmin cannot even say.

It is an especially chilly night, and Rose needs a better shelter.

She regrets not having acknowledged the girl; what if she might have a warm, soft bed under her right now, if she had only accepted the invitation? What if the invitation was genuine? What if she let her own feelings of inadequacy stand in the way of welcome?

Rose peers around a tree. She tracked the girl to her home. Torches light the windows of the house. She is trying to gather enough courage to knock on the red door.

She will do it. She will.

Rose walks resolutely toward the door. She knocks on it before she can decide otherwise. She waits.

But when White opens the door and withdraws from the doorway with a gasp, Rose knows it is much worse than she thought. She is wearing her black-gray cloak and pulls the hood closer around her face. Her hair sticks out in wiry gray ribbons; she can see it in her peripheral vision.

Red joins her sister in the doorway. When she sees Rose, she beams, and the warmth of her smile is a buoyant salve for Rose's racing heart.

"Would you care for some supper?" Red says, and she opens the door wide. She tosses her sister a significant look, as though to say, *This is the woman.* White nods and moves away with another quick glance at Rose. "My mother always prepares extra," White says.

Rose finds her voice at last. "That is very kind," she says. Her voice, surprisingly, is gentle and melodious, though a bit scratchy. She has not used it in some days. She had not noticed its youthful lilt.

Red stares at her for a long moment, then pulls Rose inside and closes the door. She says, "I am Rose-Red. Red for short." She gestures toward White. "And this is Snow-White. White for short." She smiles at Rose expectantly.

Rose says, "I am Rose." And Red beams even brighter and claps her hands.

When they sit down to dinner, Red and White's mother joins them. She has the same fair skin and pale hair as White. She says her name is Kindra.

The scene around the table is so familiar and peaceful that Rose finds her thoughts moving to her own family, her mother and father and Niram. She never dreamed that she would miss Niram, but she does. So much. And her mother, even though she was critical. And her father, even though he said nothing to balm the criticism.

She misses them all, because they were hers.

"Are you new to Eastermoor?" Kindra says.

Rose is not quite sure how to answer this question. So she says, "Somewhat."

Kindra looks at her knowingly. "The people of Eastermoor are not exactly kind to those they consider outsiders," she says. Rose feels glad that she did not venture into the village.

"Once upon a time we were new here, too," Rose says. "It is why we live in the woods."

"We have lived here for many years, though," White offers. She does not look at Rose when she speaks.

"Why do you still live in the woods?" Rose says. Her voice becomes a bit less scratchy every time she uses it. She sips her hot tea. The tension at the table changes, thickens. Perhaps she asked the wrong question.

She tries again. "Do the creatures of the woods not bother you?"

"I marked this house for protection," Kindra says. "They keep away because of it."

Rose sits up straighter. "So there is magic in this house?"

"A bit," Kindra says. "My daughters were not born with the gift of magic." Her eyes turn sad. "And I have surrendered all of mine."

"You are twins?" Rose says to the girls.

"She is a quarter hour older," Red says.

"And much wiser," White says.

Rose smiles. She always wanted a sister. A twin would be ever better.

But she also always thought twins had the strongest gifts of magic. Why were these twins born without magic if their mother had been a sorceress?

There is no more time for questions; Kindra and her daughters begin cleaning up, and talk turns to singing. They all have lovely voices, and Rose enjoys herself thoroughly. She offers her hand at chores, but they will not hear of it—she is their guest.

As they are preparing for bed, Red says, "A black wolf has been spying on me."

"You and your wild stories," Kindra says.

"And there is a beast who lives in a castle that sits in the middle of these woods," Red says.

White shakes her head and laughs. "You must stop reading so many books. Your imagination does not know what is real and what is false anymore."

Red sighs, as though these reactions are not unusual for her sister and mother. Rose feels sorry for her. She almost intervenes, to say that she has seen the same things, but it is such a sweet domestic scene that she does not feel it is her place to interrupt.

She is, after all, an outsider here.

They put her to sleep in the bed of Red and White, who will sleep by the fireside this eve. Rose tries to protest; she does not want to take anyone's bed. But Red leans forward and says, "It is a privilege," and her eyes are so merry and bright that Rose believes her.

She falls asleep nearly as soon as her head hits the down pillow.

But a noise wakens her during the night. She is still on edge, still hyper-aware of everything around her. The noise is barely there, a scraping coming from the front of the house.

Rose creeps from her bed and pauses in front of the door. She presses her hand to the jewel in the side of her nose. If it is a creature, she will be prepared.

But when she opens the front door, careful not to make a sound, she only sees Red.

"Shut the door," Red hisses.

Rose does.

"What are you doing out here?" Rose says. She can see, of course, that Red is scrubbing the top of the doorframe, but it does not make sense.

"I am wiping away the mark my mother put on this house," Red says.

"But that is a mark of protection." Rose gazes toward the woods that nearly swallow the house. She imagines hundreds of glowing eyes peering back—or does she imagine it? She shivers.

Red's dark eyes gleam in the glow of the moon that bends and fractures around the trees. Her face is dotted with pale moon glow. She says, "I think it is keeping my father away."

"Your father?" In all the conversation they had, no one mentioned a father. Of course Rose knows that Red and White have a father; she simply did not ask about him.

Red gazes up at the doorframe. "He studied Were creatures." Sadness softens her voice. "I think he might have become one. Or maybe something more."

"How can that be?" Rose does not know much about Were creatures. She has heard of them, of course; they were Niram's favorite creature. He passed a year talking incessantly about Were creatures and how he hoped to see one someday. When he ventured through such obsessions, Rose usually tuned him out. Now she wishes she had listened better.

Red lets out a long breath. "This black wolf has been following me for forty-one days," Red says. "He watches me, but he does not attack. He does not even show

himself. I only know he is there because I am perceptive."
She pauses. "It is odd, is it not?" She looks at Rose as
though Rose might have answers.

Rose has nothing, only a gripping mass of fear that is
growing by the second. "But he is a wolf," she says.
"There is no telling what he will do."

Red waves a hand, as though impatient with Rose.
"He is my father."

"How do you know?"

"You do not believe me," Red says, a note of
irritation lifting the words now. "Just like Mother and
White. Well, I will show all of you."

"You will let all the beasts of the forest come," Rose
says. "For one?"

Red's eyes shine. "Love is always worth the risk." She
flicks her head to the side. "Besides, I have my bow and
enchanted arrows." Rose looks toward the corner of the
porch, where she spies a bow and its insufficient supply
of arrows. "They never run out."

"But—"

"And with you by my side, we will keep the other
creatures away." Red has finally finished her scrubbing.
"You are a sorceress, are you not?"

Rose nearly opens her mouth to say something, but
Red holds her finger to her lips. She peers into the

darkness, squinting her eyes, then crosses the porch to her bow. She picks it up.

"It should not take them long," she says. "And we will be ready."

Rose stares at Red for a moment, a moment in which her mind turns over the possibilities. The creatures could come. They could destroy Rose and Red and White and Kindra. She and the others could vanish into nothingness, go the natural way of the woods, and no one would be the wiser.

Or…

Rose prefers the other possibility, the possibility in which she is needed. In which she has a purpose. In which she has no need for beauty and grace.

So she joins Red in the shadowed corner of the porch, her staff unfolded and outstretched, and they wait for the unknown, together.

As friends might do.

# Becoming

It was, in actuality, only a fortnight that Mira spent learning all she could about magic. Not even a moon had passed before Mira knocked on the doors of Fairendale castle. They were opened—both of them flung with a grunt and a sigh—by a gruff man in a blue tunic and brown breeches, with boots of the same color and shade as the breeches. He had milky blue eyes, the kind of eyes that either cannot see a thing or can see and sense everything, and a shock of white hair on the sides of his head, but none at the top.

"We do not hand out gifts to villagers," he said, already closing the heavy oak doors.

"I have come to inquire if I might be needed at the castle," Mira said, shoving one foot inside one of the doors. She was a large woman, and the man was bony and small.

His eyes widened. "Needed for what?" he said.

"I am a very skilled cook," she said. She was not. She had never cooked a thing in her life, but she had the gift of magic.

This she did not say.

"We have a cook already," the man said, and he began to shut the door again. Mira's foot did not move.

"I am willing to be an assistant first," she said. She arched one of her eyebrows. She knew that she was still young and beautiful, and men were predictable when it came to youth and charm. "But I believe you will want me in charge soon."

It was a bold claim, but the man, after some hesitation, finally opened the door and introduced her to the castle manager, who, as a young man, took to her immediately. Predictably. Mira was glad for her long red-brown locks and her pale blue eyes, fringed with dark lashes. She could change her appearance to whatever she wanted it to be. This was one of the gifts of her shape shifting—not only that she could become a bear at will, but that she could also shift the color of her eyes and the shape of her nose and the shade of her skin. She could wear an entirely different face, and from what she knew of magic, what she had learned from the stone that spoke with Bregdon's voice, this was quite extraordinary.

She chose, however, to wear her original eyes and nose and skin. In case Anthony returned. It was an endless and ever-present hope.

Her powers of magic were strong, yes, but as soon as she crossed the threshold of Fairendale castle, their warm fever-like presence became an inferno. Mira looked around at the walls, lined with the portraits of past royal families, and she knew that these walls could not hold her. They *would* not hold her.

She was free.

Mira bowed her head and thanked Bregdon, who was likely watching over her—though, truth be told, Bregdon was on the other side of the realm, searching for a missing prophet who had been integral to many of the happenings in the realm. He had not been paying attention to Mira at all. He had left her in good hands—the hands of the white stone—and that was that.

Time passed, and Mira went about her duties and continued waiting—for what, she did not know. But she had always been good at waiting, and this was no exception.

Mira became an assistant to the cook, and when the cook was dismissed, she stepped up the ranks.

Mira became Cook.

# Resistance

It is a very long time before the creatures come. Red and Rose watch them gather—first, the more well-known creatures: more wild boars, large gray wolves, snakes of every kind; next, the lesser known creatures: trolls, goblins, even what looked like a massive spider. Were they Were creatures or simply creatures? Rose looks up at the moon. It is not yet full.

A growl sounds and then echoes down the line, filling the night sky. The front door opens.

"Red." It is the only word Kindra presses out before a gasp steals whatever else she might say. Her eyes flick to Rose, the blue barely containing the storm. "What have you done?"

Rose tries to say something, anything, to let Kindra know she would never, ever put them in danger. But she is only an ugly crone. Why would Kindra believe her?

And now look what has happened.

White appears in the doorway, her face the same color as the moonlight. "Why are they here, Mother?" she whispers, her eyes wide and wet.

"They have been called," Kindra says, and in those words Rose can hear all the contempt she should have expected from a stranger. She let her guard down. She allowed herself to hope.

"I called them," Red says into the stillness that follows. Kindra's head jerks toward her daughter. Her eyes widen. "I removed the protective mark." Red says the words as though they are perfectly rational; as though there is not an army of creatures gathering against four females, three of whom, if Kindra and White are like Rose, have never fought a single one; as though anyone would have done the same in her position.

Rose nearly bursts out laughing. Fear is the shaky sister of mirth.

"You…" Kindra's whisper trails off. She looks back at the gathering creatures and shakes her head. "But you have doomed us all. That mark is the only thing that kept the creatures at bay."

"And Father, too," Red says.

Kindra looks from Red back to the throng and back

to Red. "Your father is not a forest creature." Her voice is high, firm, but slightly panicked.

"I think he may be," Rose says, without looking at her mother.

The creatures begin their advance, as though a hand signaled them to do so. They creep, slowly, closer and closer, testing the boundaries, moving like a wall of danger, until Rose knows that she will have to do what no one else will be able to do. She will have to defend Red, Kindra, and White from these creatures. With magic.

"I might be able to hold them off," Rose says over the din of gnashing and growling. "And allow you time to escape."

"But this is our home," Kindra says. It is not logical; it is emotional.

"And it is overrun with creatures," Rose says. She keeps her words gentle, open, understanding.

"And what will you do?" Red says. She has moved beside Rose, positioned an arrow, and drawn the bow taut. "You need me as well."

"No," Rose says. "You must go."

Red does not listen. She remains where she is.

"Go," Rose says.

Red does not appear to hear her. She pulls the string tighter and closes one eye. "I have not known you for long," she says at last. "But friends do not need time, only devotion." And she looses an arrow, which heads straight into the eye of a boar. It falls. The creatures pick up their pace.

Rose is nearly overcome by the emotion of what she has heard, but she lifts her staff and closes her eyes and whispers her spell.

She hears White say, "Why are they so angry?" and Kindra say, "Because we have evaded them for so long." She hears Red shriek and the arrows whistle from the bow. She hears the growls and stomps and hisses of the creatures.

"Wait." It is the voice of Red that opens Rose's eyes. The creatures hold still now, as though frozen in place by some unknown force. Was it her magic?

In front of the creatures is a large black wolf. It stands far enough away but close enough to see its earth-brown eyes glittering in the gleaming light of the moon.

"Father," Red breathes.

Rose looks at the wolf. The wolf draws closer, the only creature moving, and Rose raises her staff. But just before she curls her voice around another spell, a beautiful woman in a flowing green dress steps around the side of the house, into her peripheral view.

She knows this woman. She has seen this woman

before. She is the Enchantress who gave her—and all the other lost children of Fairendale—a home inside the Weeping Woods. A shoe-shaped home.

"You might want to swallow that spell of yours," the woman says, and she points her staff toward Rose. A tiny tendril of green darts straight at Rose's heart. Red tries to launch herself in front of Rose with a shrieking "No!" But she is too late. The tendril slams into Rose's chest, and she feels a pinching in her fingers and toes, and then she knows no more.

The Enchantress lifts her hand, and the small black bird that used to be Rose alights on her palm. She runs her fingertips over the shining head of the bird and then turns her attention to the three women.

"It is better this way," she says.

The wolf behind her growls, and she smiles before turning her attention to him. "I know what you are," she says, and she sends another coil of green, this one large and thick, toward him. It stretches into a fog that covers him, and when it clears he is a man with a broad chest and cherrywood hair and eyes the color of wet earth, all of which can be seen by the light of the beaming moon.

It is a happy ending for four people in this tale—except for a small caveat. Red and White's father, whose name is Orville, is bound to the forest. He can never leave it. Which means, if the family wishes to remain a family, they can never leave it, either.

The Enchantress delivers this news in a most matter-of-fact way.

The family members all look at one another. No one says a word.

Red glares at the Enchantress, but she has, the Enchantress notices, the good sense to keep quiet as well. The Enchantress can feel her dislike, but sorceresses were not made to be loved.

Still, she feels it pinch her chest.

She believes her work here is done, until the girl impertinently says, "What have you done with Rose?"

The Enchantress tilts her head. She is about to answer when the Huntsman rounds the corner of the house, dressed to look like a human tree. It is as ridiculous as it ever was. The Enchantress does not introduce him, merely ignores him until he hands her the iron cage, in which she places the blackbird.

"Rose is now our charge," the Enchantress says.

"But why?" Red says. "Why do you want her?"

The Enchantress heaves out a long breath. She has

been fortunate in these last weeks to not have met another child like Red. Questions weary her like nothing else.

Well, except for her expenditure of magic. She can feel the exhaustion puddling behind her eyes.

"She is in a safer place," the Enchantress says.

"Give her back," Red says.

The Enchantress allows herself to laugh. She feels the Huntsman's eyes on her face. "Why would you care about a silly old crone?" she says.

Red's face registers confusion. Is it the question that has confused her or something else? When the girl opens her mouth to speak, the Enchantress understand her confusion. "She was a child," Red says.

The Enchantress feels a snake of alarm slither into her chest. She has heard of those who can see through magic. What about her own? She gathers all the courage that remains and says, "She was an old crone, and nothing more."

Red shakes her head and looks at her mother and sister. "She was a child," she says. "It is why she needed us."

Fortunately, her mother and sister look at her as though she is mad.

The Enchantress stares at Red for a moment, and

then she turns away, before the girl can peel away her mask as well. "I have protected your home," the Enchantress throws over her shoulder. "You have no need to worry about the creatures anymore."

"But you are a child, too." Red's words twist into the air, fold around the Enchantress's shoulders, and smother the breath from her chest.

"You are mistaken," she says to the woods. She does not turn.

"But—"

"Enough, Red." The girl's mother steps in at last. The Enchantress turns and smiles now. There is something else she must say, something else Red and White must know, something else that throbs in her chest.

"I have given back your father," the Enchantress says. "But you must know that a girl without a father is still a strong, capable, precious girl."

She leaves them with that. She does not see the mother and father and the two girls fall into one another's arms. She does not see the worried look that crosses the face of the mother when she looks at her dark daughter. She does not see them move into their home, together, for the first time in ten years.

What she does see are the eyes of the Huntsman, fixed on her with a hundred unanswerable questions, the loudest of which is, *A child?*

Fortunately, the magic pulls down a black curtain over her mind and her eyes and her body. She crumples to the forest floor, where the Huntsman will carry her to the cart and cover her with his coat of many colors. It has become a ritual of sorts. But this time something is different.

This time there is doubt.

This time there is a question: *A child?*

Iddo is still trying to escape his secret work shop, which is carved into the ground, outside his small cottage in the woods of Lincastle. He has been trying to escape for what seems like a very long time now.

He has been trapped in this underground laboratory, where he once trapped Yasmin, since someone closed and locked the doors on him—his own security system turned against him. They are as impenetrable as he had intended when he chained a man-made monster in this room. He had not wanted her to escape, and now he is unable to escape.

Fortunately, he has managed to rummage around in the complete darkness (the everlasting candle was not something the monster left for him, sadly, and his own torches burned out long ago, nearly as soon as he entered this chamber and the door slammed shut on him). He has, by touch, located his compartment beneath the floor, in which he once hid emergency supplies. He would have been foolish to not consider that something like this would happen someday (though he clearly had not believed it *would* happen, or he would have built in an alternate escape). He now has another everlasting candle lighting his space. Light brings hope.

But none of his tools have worked on the locks.

None of his tools have worked on his thoughts, either.

Who set the monster free? She was not able to free herself; someone must have known. His mind, in the days since his own imprisonment, have run over the list. The boy might have known, years ago, when Iddo took his dead mother and attempted to raise her back to life. But the boy had grown, had become a king, had died.

Someone else, then?

He stole some things from the Evil Queen over the years; in fact, this candle had been hers. He justified his night burglaries by telling himself he did not intend to keep whatever he took; he only meant to borrow it. For a few years. In some cases, a couple of decades.

Perhaps she knew and had come for her revenge.

She had several everlasting candles in her cottage, though. She would not have missed one or two.

But what about the pages he copied of the Old Man's Great Book? If his memory serves him, he left one of those copied pages in his haste to leave one night when the Evil Queen returned home unexpectedly.

Had she known about his treachery, then?

He does not know why his thoughts circle the Evil Queen. They occasionally passed each other in the streets of Lincastle, but they never spoke. She always gave him a strange look, one that said, "Do I know you?" And he always wanted to say, emphatically, "No."

He felt close to his father in her cottage. He cannot say why.

Iddo has no concept of what time it is. He does not know what day it is, nor how many days he has been locked in this miserable work space (he would be surprised to know that it has been, in fact, six days—nearly seven; he would guess it has been more. Time stretches and expands when locked in a prison.).

He is growing tired of searching for a way out.

He is simply growing tired.

He is a very old man. What would it matter if he died here? No one depends on him anymore; no one has depended on him for a very long time. It was a good life, was it not? Perhaps he should lie down and sleep.

But someone does depend on him—the entire realm. For protection. The enchantment is entrusted to Iddo alone. He does not have the gift of magic anymore, but he is permitted to do this one thing: keep Fairendale invisible to those sailing the Violet Sea, and vice versa.

And though he does not know how many days he has been locked in this work shop, he knows it has been too many.

He should have passed along the responsibility years ago. He should have known it would end this way.

Iddo lies down, his cheek against the cold floor.

Fairendale will be noticed. Invaders will come. Iddo will have failed the realm—and it is this for which he will be known.

He closes his eyes.

A voice inside him, however, will not allow him to give up. It says, *Go on. Keep trying.*

It sounds like the voice of his father. Iddo never really liked his father; he pushed Iddo too hard, expected him to be perfect. Iddo had been rather glad when his father had mysteriously disappeared and never turned up again.

An unexpected swell of emotion blurs his vision. Iddo shakes his head and blinks his eyes. He swallows hard.

He built this place to be impenetrable, and

impenetrable it is. How ironic that the one thing he did perfectly is the one thing that may very well kill him.

Iddo examines the door again. Yasmin must have had help getting out. Someone must have closed the door on him.

Who?

Who might have been able to break his locks in the first place? He collected all sorts of science to make this place what it is.

He leans his head back against the wall. His mind has grown cloudy. He needs something to eat. He ran out of emergency food provisions, too. Why did he not think to pack more? He thought he could escape in so little time? From an impenetrable room?

Iddo shakes his head. He really is a foolish man.

For hydration, Iddo has been drinking potions. He knows it is not wise, knows they are more poison than anything else (he is, after all, the one who made them), but what does a man do when there is nothing else to drink and the body is desperate?

He hopes the end will be swift.

He closes his eyes.

Something scratches across the floor. He opens his eyes.

It is a pitcher of water. Iddo looks at it, blinks, licks

his lips. It must be his imagination. It must be. The pitcher he kept for Yasmin was empty when he got here, and now it is filled.

The poison is doing its work. He is imagining what he most desires. Good. He closes his eyes again. The scratching sound peels them open. The water container is closer than it was before, is it not?

Iddo leans forward.

He really must be at the end.

He closes his eyes, for the last time, he thinks. The scratching is brief and louder. The water pitcher is within reach, vibrating, glowing.

Glowing?

Iddo touches it. It is real. It is full. He pours a drink into a beaker and gulps it down. He pours another and gulps it down, too. He pours another and another, and the pitcher never empties.

So he will live. Or he has already died.

Iddo looks around. No one is here. Fear claws at his too-filled stomach.

And then the candle goes out, the same candle that is made to burn forever and ever and ever.

Darkness wins.

The Graces make lovely music. They have never done this before, but it does not feel that way. It feels as though they have never done anything else.

Mirth plucks the strings of a harp. Good Cheer plays a flute. Splendor sings.

Night breathes around them.

It is the Summoning Song. It is an enchanted melody that will drift across the lands and be heard by only those who are Summoned, which, in this case, are the shape shifters—the six of them in the realm of Fairendale. And once the music reaches them, beckons them, they will come. Or they are expected to come. This is the purpose of the shape shifters: to join their cause with the Graces, to protect the land, to heal it, if need be.

These shape shifters are summoned for a purpose greater than whatever it is they do in their separate places. They will now join together to save the Great Tree of Helomoth.

The song rises. It is a song as old as time, a song they have never known and yet have always known, a song that will save the world, perhaps.

The Graces sing and dance and play until the sun breaks forth from the horizon. And then they wait.

And across the land, the shape shifters lift their heads.

They rub their ears. They listen.

They know.

They are being Summoned.

It is time to go.

Three of them take off running—two bears and a cat.

One stares at the sky.

Another lifts her chin.

And the third turns away.

These will take their moment. Perhaps they will ignore the call altogether.

Mira touches the brass knocker on the door marking the entrance to Fairendale castle. The knocker is fashioned in the image of a bear, her shape shifting form. It must mean something. It is the image her brother put on this door. He must have known that she, his sister, was half bear, half woman.

Perhaps he was half-bear, too.

She closes her eyes. She would have liked to have known her brother. She would have liked to save him from the king who stole the throne. She would have liked to...

Well, there is no sense in reminiscing. What was done is done. She has something to do.

She is performing her customary Protection spell to maintain the invisible fortress around Fairendale castle and its people, as she has done every day since she returned. She does not know if it works anymore or not, considering the monster-woman who is currently sitting on the throne. Still she tries. She would rather do too much work than too little.

Mira has already finished her walk around the castle. She has watched the green tendrils crimp toward the castle's stone walls. She has felt the magic leaving her and exhaustion replacing it in waves.

The tinkling of a bell makes her tilt her head, curve it to the south. She hears music. She looks around. She is alone.

The music grows louder, more insistent.

She has never heard this song before.

But she knows it.

It is as old as time.

Mira is being Summoned.

The tug on the strings of the apron she wears around her dress is nearly overwhelming, but Mira resists it. She will change into her bear skin, but not by someone else's insistence, not right now. She must see the boy first. She must tell him where she is going this time. She must tell him everything.

And give him something.

Mira's heart throbs. She will have to leave the boy again. She may not come back. But she will give him everything he needs. She will tell him that she believes he can do what he thinks he cannot do. She will say what needs saying.

First Mira turns to the garden, waving her magic across the plants, ensuring their abundant yield in her absence. Then she closes her eyes and directs a spell toward the dungeons beneath the dungeons, where children and prophets wake and sleep and long for freedom; this spell will sustain them, in case of disaster.

And then Mira turns to the castle. She throws back her head and summons the wind, feels it on the tips of her fingers, releases it toward the ramparts and balustrades. She flings her hands out to her side, letting loose every bit of magic she has, for now. The wind roars around her, a storm awakening.

She pours herself into this final Protection spell.

Mira crumples on the ground.

But she will wake. And when she does, she will go in search of the boy. She will find him in the kitchen. She will give him what he most needs to survive what is asked of him: she will give him hope.

It is the earliest part of the morning, and King Willis is still King Willis. The real King Willis. Nothing has gotten past the spell Mira—Cook—has faithfully cooked into his meals (mostly soup), using an enchanted pot. Not even the throne's magic has cracked it, though King Willis has sat on this cursed throne every day and every night.

Perhaps a strong spell combined with a strong will—which King Willis used to have and seems to have rediscovered—is the perfect cure for a curse.

That King Willis is still the real King Willis is a fortunate thing.

If Queen Clarion were here, peering into the throne room, she would be glad to know it. Unfortunately, she assumes, wrongly, that her husband has succumbed, once more, to the curse, and she has locked herself in the castle library, where she is desperately trying to find a way to beat the throne's influence—a search that will be needed in the coming days, but not for the purpose she thinks: saving King Willis. King Willis has been saved by Mira.

King Willis has been saved by himself.

When King Willis entered the throne room last evening, after consuming his supper, he found Yasmin leaving it. She has not left him alone in several days, so her departure was unexpected. Yasmin, it seems, has gone off in search of something. Of what King Willis does not know. He cannot even guess, though he is afraid he might have heard a mutter that indicated she intends to find Queen Clarion.

Queen Clarion has magic. King Willis hopes his wife will be able to take care of herself.

Yasmin has been gone for some time—all night. King Willis slept fitfully, dreaming of Yasmin's return. But when he woke, she was still gone. King Willis does not know when to expect her back. He tries to focus on the opportunity that is before him.

He may not have another chance.

Now he is given a moment to himself, a moment to think, a moment to stand beside the throne and consider its destruction.

He kicks it, which only serves to damage his foot. He hisses in a breath and hops a bit, nearly tumbling off the stage. He sits down heavily and gazes at the golden legs. He saw it glowing once, did he not? A violet color. What does it mean?

There is still so much about magic he does not know or understand. His brother, Wendell, tried to teach him, and King Willis attempted, for a time, to learn on his own after Wendell was banished by their father, King Sebastien. But one does not truly know magic unless one possesses the gift.

He is at a significant disadvantage in this. He never had the gift.

King Willis glances toward the front doors of the throne room. He tried to leave the night before this one, while the monster slept soundly on a large bed she moved to the corner of the stage, heavy red curtains hiding her from view. He was knocked so roughly back from the doors—as though something had collided with his chest—that he could hardly keep to his feet. His breath turned to gasps, and he willed himself quiet so the monster would not wake. She did not.

She trapped him here. And if he is trapped, he must figure out how best to use that trap for good.

King Willis has shrunk in the days since the curse released its hold on him. He is still tall and broad, but he is no longer as wide. His clothes hang now. He straightens them and straightens his back, too.

It is good to be his own person again. He never wants to be anyone else.

And yet there is so much pain. There is his brother (where is he?); there are the children in the dungeons (how are they, and how can he set them free?); there is his son (when will he see him again?). But King Willis stands, straight-backed, chin lifted, and allows the pain the roll over his shoulders and down his chest and into his belly. He allows the tears to blur his eyes, stream down his cheeks, pool at his collar. He breathes. He feels. He is himself.

He calls out, "Garth!" and the boy comes running, though it is much too early in the morning. Perhaps Garth, too, was uneasy with Yasmin's absence and never went to bed.

Garth comes and goes through the throne room doors with no problem. And if the boy is the only one who can come and go, besides the monster, King Willis will use him. No, not use him—include him.

"I have need of some parchment," King Willis says. "Six pieces. And a pen and some ink." Garth nods and begins to move away. King Willis adds, "Make haste, and take care." Garth stops, stares at his king for a minute, and turns away. King Willis smiles.

Yes. He is himself.

He is a king who can remember names. He is a king with mercy. He is a king who loves.

Love is a dangerous, ridiculous thing.

Garth returns in nearly no time at all and hands King Willis a piece of parchment and a feather quill pen, along with a bottle of black ink. "My table," King Willis says.

Garth brings him a small foldable table, which King Willis sets in front of the throne. He sits in the throne carefully, as though unsure whether the curse will, at any moment, claim him again, but he feels none of its cold. He lets out a breath and smooths out the parchment. He dips the pen into the ink and begins to write.

He writes one letter after another.

When he is finished, he rolls up the parchment pieces and ties them with some brown thread that Garth pulled from his pocket. Garth hands him some hot wax and a metal stamp. King Willis marks each letter with the official Fairendale seal, a bear standing on two feet. "Send this straightaway to all the other lands, one to each," he says, handing over the six rolls.

Garth nods and hurries off. King Willis settles back into the throne.

He has written a letter calling off the search for the lost children of Fairendale, entreating the people of other kingdoms to keep the lost children safe until such a time when they can return to their homes—which is not now. He does not want the children handed over to him, not with a monster here in the castle of Fairendale. Not even if there were no monster in the castle. He would still not want them. In his clear-minded state, King Willis knows that he has no need of a throne he cannot keep; if there is a magical boy, perhaps it would better for the throne to be his. King Willis never wanted to rule in the first place. It was his father's doing that kept him here. His father and the throne.

What did he plan to do with the children? He cannot remember.

King Willis sits up. He must find a way to release the captives in the dungeons beneath the dungeons. They cannot continue on, locked away from all those who love them.

Perhaps then the kingdom will be well on its way to restoration. Perhaps the village people will release his son. Perhaps he and Queen Clarion and Prince Virgil can live their own happily ever after, outside a castle, in another land. His thoughts turn dreamy. His hands settle on the arms of the throne. He stares at its elegance. It is a beautiful throne. One cannot tell, before sitting on it, just how evil it is.

Why does its curse not work on him now? Is it his will or something else? And does that have an expiration date? Will he one day discover that he has once again lost control of himself? Or is he strong enough to resist?

King Willis hopes. And hope is enough for today.

In the castle mail room, Garth attaches the letters of the king to the legs of pigeons that will carry them to their intended places. One to Lincastle, one to Eastermoor, one to White Wind, one to Rosehaven, one to Ashvale (in case any people remain), and one, even, to Guardia, where it is said only savages live (though these tales are not entirely true).

But just after the pigeons take flight, when they reach the spot in the Weeping Woods where they would all go their separate ways—some to the north, some east, some west, one south—each of them falls from the sky, at the same time. They drop into a pigeon pile, unable to move.

Someone has intercepted the messages.

The letters will never reach their intended destinations.

And Fairendale will be all the worse for it.

**Don't miss the next Fairendale adventure!**
Find out what happens when a boy must choose between being a monster or a hero in Book 15: *The Boy Who Frightened Miss Muffet.*

# An Interview with Rose

## Transcribed by L.R. Patton
## Author


**L.R.:** It is so good to have you here, Rose, though I must confess, it is difficult to see you with that haze over your face.

**Rose:** Haze? I am sorry, I do not know to what you refer.

**L.R.:** Can you see all right?

**Rose:** Very well. I can see that you are right in front of me, and you have fair skin and muddy-colored—

**L.R.:** Oh! That is all very well. I simply could not… cannot…see you all that clearly. It looks as though you have a haze covering your face. I cannot tell if you have fully recovered from the Vanishing spell.

**Rose:** I do not think I am at liberty to say.

**L.R.:** What makes you think that, dear?

**Rose:** Because of the mfulplsd

**L.R.:** I am afraid we did not understand you. Could you, perhaps, repeat what you said?

**Rose:** No, I cannot. Please move on to another question.

**L.R.:** Very well. [Long pause.] Okay. So tell me about this desire of yours to become a scribe. How long have you had such plans?

**Rose:** Since I learned to write at five.

**L.R.:** It is a fun profession.

**Rose:** I enjoy it very much.

**L.R.:** And it was very creative, the way you made those bark books and etched your stories into them. I am sure it took quite a bit of time.

**Rose:** I had quite a bit of time on my hands.

**L.R.:** Yes, I suppose you did. [Under breath] What I would give for uninterrupted time like that.

**Rose:** I am sorry? I did not hear you.

**L.R.:** Nothing, dear. What sorts of things did you learn in the woods of Eastermoor?

**Rose:** Oh, ever so much. I learned that creatures are around every corner—and some of them are quite hideous, that friends can be found in unlikely places, and that insects do not taste all that bad when you cover them with chocolate.

**L.R.:** That last lesson: are you sure?

**Rose:** They are quite nutritious.

**L.R.:** Yes, but nutritious does not always translate to tasty.

**Rose:** Everything is tasty when wrapped in chocolate. Grasshoppers, locusts, ants, inchworms—

**L.R.:** You did not really eat a worm, did you?

**Rose:** You would be surprised at what you will eat when you wish to stay alive.

**L.R.:** Tell us what you thought when you saw your

reflection—your transformed one—in the water.

**Rose:** I thought I was hideous.

**L.R.:** Why?

**Rose:** Because I lost my hair and my eyes and my smooth skin. I lost my youth. I was someone entirely different.

**L.R.:** Did you learn anything significant, then?

**Rose:** That beauty is superficial. A girl does not need beauty to have worth. She has worth simply because she exists.

**L.R.:** That is a profound lesson.

**Rose:** Yes, well, undesirable circumstances often teach us profound lessons, do they not?

**L.R.:** Are you sure you are only twelve?

**Rose:** I will soon be thirteen, though I have lost count of the months. Perhaps I am already thirteen.

**L.R.:** Are you glad for the transformation?

**Rose:** I am glad for what I learned. And for meeting Rose-Red.

**L.R.:** Are you and Rose-Red still friends, then?

**Rose:** I believe my time is up. Here comes my mfulplsd

**L.R.:** Here comes your what? I think something might have gone wrong with your mouth momentarily. I could not understand you.

**Rose:** Goodbye for now!

**L.R.:** Wait. Rose?

**Rose:**

**L.R.:** [long, loud sigh.] I wonder, dear reader, when we will manage to get any information out of these fairy tale children. I confess I am growing weary of trying and watching it end the same way every time. Perhaps next time I will attempt a new strategy and see if we might take by surprise whoever is holding the children. What do you think of that?

In the meantime (there is no way of knowing how much meantime will pass), if you would like to read more Fairendale extras like this interview, be sure to visit www.lrpatton.com/fairendale.

# Things to Do When Trapped in a Tower

**By Mira, also known as Cook**
**Cook, Castle Manager, and Castle Guardian**
**at Fairendale Castle**


It seems that it is not so uncommon as it used to be for certain fathers or husbands or a random enemy to lock a female in a tower. Though I am in favor of a female doing whatever she can to break free of a tower prison, I must admit that sometimes the circumstances call for one to remain patient and (mostly) content within the tower.

If you find yourself in that position—if, perhaps, your confinement is something milder, such as being confined to your room for days on end because you have done something that your parents did not find as humorous as you thought it might be (for example: breaking a light with an ill-placed potato), here are some helpful ways to pass the time:

### 1. Sing

Music has been proven to make the mind and heart feel better. Something about the melody lifts the spirits of one who is trapped (or otherwise in a state of disappointment or despair). This is why, oftentimes, I would pace around my tower cell singing continuously.

You can create your own songs or you can sing the songs you remember your mother singing to you when you were a baby. You can sing the songs that birds perform outside your window (they enjoy it when you sing back to them), or the song the wind carries to you upon a breeze. There are many songs in the world and many ways in which to sing them. Never stop singing.

**2. Bury yourself in stories**

Stories always help pass time—whether you are waiting for a celebration to start or you are stuck in a tower (or, perhaps, a cell, as our unfortunate prophets and some of the Fairendale children are). Stories can be read, if there is access to books, and also imagined. I created many fantastical stories when I was locked in my tower on the Varena Isles. Unfortunately I did not have anything with which to write, so all my stories have now left me. I can remember none of them now. But I am sure if you have a captor who visits you frequently or if you are not so captive as I was, you will have better access to some parchment and a pen so you can record your stories. It seems that when the mind is unstimulated from the world around you, it can create all kinds of things. You never know what you might come up with. Sometimes it may be worth locking yourself in your room, posting a "keep out" sign on your door, just for the pleasure of silence and stories. I hear that is what our narrator does.

### 3. Draw

When I was trapped in my tower, I would pass many comfortable hours drawing on my walls. My father believed in the arts and kept a great store of supplies in one of the castle storage rooms; I had my maidservant sneak up some paints for me. I would spend hours every day painting the walls with grand murals, starting all over again when I ran out of space. I am told it is not recommended for others to paint on walls, so perhaps, for you, it would be wise to collect a notebook or some paper before you begin drawing. But I am also told it is not wise to draw only one thing on a piece of paper—one should create an entire scene with that paper before moving on to another drawing. It is great practice to envision what a scene looks like, using the imagination, rather than simply drawing a spider in the middle of a page and calling it done.

If you were to see my walls, you would not be able to distinguish one scene from another; I painted so many, filled every space, tried to infuse my prison with color.

I was trapped in my tower for a very long time.

### 4. Pace

One may wonder how a woman could exercise enough to stimulate the heart and remain healthy when she is locked in a circular tower. While my tower was quite spacious, I understand that not everyone's is. But there are still some simple things one can do to keep the heart and body healthy: what I call Scissor Jumps, Duck Walk, Wall Pushes, and Frog Jumps are some recommendations. There are too many to list here, I am afraid.

Or, if one is disinclined to work up a sweat, one could simply pace. Even if your tower is only large enough for five or so steps (this is also motivation to keep your tower clean and free of clutter), you can still effectively walk back and forth, back and forth, as fast as you would like. For extra stimulation, pace on your toes or with your knees bent or even backward.

Suffice it to say that just because you are locked in a tower does not mean your activity should end.

### 5. Observe

Most towers are equipped with a window. You would be surprised at the kinds of things you can see from a tower window. I saw ships sailing into the harbor, I saw birds engaging in their migratory patterns, I saw storms rolling in, I saw people whispering in the streets, I saw who was doing what and formed my conclusions, even warned my father about some things.

I would sit for hours at my window, watching the comings and goings of the castle. My father did not have many visitors, but when he did, I would watch their entrance and exit. I could tell by the way they walked why they had come and what my father had said to their request. They were suitors, and my father turned them all away. This leads me to believe that, in the end, he heard my wishes: I did not want to marry any one of them. I suppose that makes me feel grateful to him for at least not asking me to marry someone I could not love.

If you find yourself locked inside a tower, I hope you do not regard it with too much hopelessness. You must remember you will not always be locked in a tower—no one is—and, in the meantime, there is plenty to do to keep your mind and heart engaged.

You are limited only by your imagination.

# How to Know a Grace Has Influenced You

**By L.R. Patton**
**Author**

Many letters have reached me in recent days in which readers wonder how they might tell whether they have been influenced by a Grace. Since the Graces are invisible to people squarely in the living realm, it is practically impossible to tell when they are working on you. But here are some ways to know that your life has been visited by a Grace.

**1. You forget what you were saying in the middle of saying it.**

Some people believe that if you forget what you were saying in the middle of it, that means what you were about to say was not all that important. This is actually impossible to know. Perhaps what you were about to say would have influenced someone in a way that would change the world for the worse, and a Grace stepped in because she thought you needed a little guidance. Or perhaps what you were about to say might have been misconstrued by the person to whom you were speaking, and the Grace helped you retain a friendship by allowing you to forget what you were talking about. It is anyone's guess, really. The only thing that you can know for sure is that a Grace likely took your words and released them to the wind and you are better off without them.

**2. You walk into a room and forget why.**

Have you ever entered a room and completely forgotten why you went there in the first place? This happens to me all the time. I will walk all the way up my stairs (I have a two-story house; on a side note, stairs are dangerous. Once I fell down my stairs and broke my foot. I am much more careful about going up and down them now, and I also do not like going up them if I do not really need to). I will be so excited about whatever it was for which I climbed up the stairs, and I will walk into the room and stare blankly at the walls. Sometimes I remember the Graces, but other times I wonder if someone is playing a cruel joke on me, trying to get me to walk up and down the stairs pointlessly.

It is highly likely, if this happens to you, that a Grace has stolen your memory, for one reason or another.

**3. You plan to do something and it doesn't work out.**

Sometimes your parents will announce that you're all going to do something fun for the day, and you get your hopes up, you get excited, and, to your disappointment, it does not happen the way they said it would. Some children will secretly (or vocally) think their parents were lying about their plans, but in reality, a Grace has influenced the day.

So the next time you are disappointed by something your parents say you will do in a day and it does not happen exactly the way they planned, just remember that it is likely the fault of a Grace, who has orchestrated the world so that it falls in line with not only what is best for you but also what is best for others. Perhaps, if your parents had succeeded in taking you to the children's museum, you would have gotten onto an elevator that was supposed to open on the second floor, but it did not open and you were trapped inside for an hour. Or perhaps they said they would like to take you to the zoo, but the day you do not get to go as planned, an alligator escapes his exhibit. Or the day you are disappointed you did not get to go to the park, you hear on the news that all the park benches were covered in bird poop from the flock flying by while all the children were playing (the children wore poop home, too), and you will be glad you did not visit because it saved your favorite purple shirt for another day.

**4. You make a bad decision and something terrible happens.**

If you take something from your brother and then start running away, only to slam into a wall that appeared right in front of you, as though from thin air, you can be sure that a Grace has orchestrated the circumstances to return your thievery with a consequence: the pain of a wall collision. If you are standing on a chair and your mother tells you to sit down but you ignore her and continue standing and then you fall down and hurt your rump, it is likely a Grace who has orchestrated that. If you roll your eyes when your mother tells you to clean your room and the next second you trip over something on your floor and puncture your knee on a book, you can blame the Graces.

**5. You change your mind about something but are unable to explain it.**

This happened to me recently. I was adamant about not allowing my children to do certain things on the trampoline, and then my mind flipped, as though it were connected to a switch. I could not explain this change, but I simply went with it. After all, the Graces know best, as far as I can tell.

Though it is difficult to see the influence that Graces have in our lives, their influence can be trusted. If you forget what you were saying in the middle of saying it, do not try to remember. If you forget why you came into a room, do not let it bother you. If you plan something that does not go exactly according to plan, let it be. If you find yourself making a bad decision, stop, think, and turn it around before the Graces exact their natural consequences. If you change your mind, do not question why.

The Graces are working for the world's renewal and restoration. It is in our best interest to let them.

# Insects Worth Trying at Least Once

**By Rose**

**Future scribe of Fairendale (only do not tell my parents)**

It will come as no surprise, after having read my story, that I did not fare well in the woods outside Eastermoor. I am no hunter, and though I may have managed to snag a fish had the wild boar not decided to use that moment for an attack, I did not have much opportunity to eat anything besides insects.

Which actually do not taste as bad as you might think. Though I wrapped mine in chocolate, I am told that many around the world eat insects daily. They are a good source of protein and are less harmful to the environment than animals.

Here are some of my favorite insects to eat:

Beetles (easy to catch, and they have more protein than most other insects.)

Butterflies and moths (if you can manage to eat them; some of them are much too beautiful.)

Bees and wasps (you may have to use a little magic with them, so you can avoid their sting; they are not happy about the possibility of becoming someone's chocolate-covered lunch. I speak from experience.)

Ants (they do not require much effort, especially if you find them on a mission. They will line up for you with hardly a thought.)

Grasshoppers, crickets, and locusts (they will make the most noise in the process of catching, which, if you are sensitive, could make you feel guilty.)

Flies and mosquitoes (I thought I could not stomach eating such insects, but it turns out when you are stuck in the woods and they have unlimited access to you, you will eat them just to decrease their irritating number.)

Water insects (you can find them on the surface of water, though they are difficult to catch)

Stinkbugs (once you get past their smell, they have an apple flavor. Chocolate covered apples? Yes, please.)

Bon appétit!

# The Royal Family of Fairendale

**King Willis:** The current king of Fairendale. Son of King Sebastien. Has a deep love for sweet rolls.

**Queen Clarion:** The current queen of Fairendale. Is underestimated by her husband and most of the kingdom, but she will prove just how powerful she is in due time.

**Prince Virgil:** Son of King Willis and Queen Clarion, best friend of Theo. Prefers rye bread with melted butter to sweet rolls, depending on the day. Currently exists as a blackbird, transformed by the sorceress Cora.

**King Sebastien:** Deceased king of Fairendale, exception to the line of boys who tried to steal thrones and were, upon failing at their quest, forever banished. Was killed by a blackbird. Now lives, as much as the dead can live, inside a magic mirror.

## The Former Royal Family of Fairendale

**The Good King Brendon**: Former king of Fairendale responsible for the alliance between the people of Fairendale and the dragons of Morad, lost the throne when it was stolen by King Sebastien. Killed in the Great Battle.

**Queen Marion:** Wife of the Good King Brendon, died mysteriously when her daughter was very young. Now lives in Lincastle and is "affectionately" called the Evil Queen.

**Princess Maren:** Daughter of the Good King Brendon and Queen Marion. She has been missing since the Great Battle.

## The Villagers of Fairendale

**Arthur:** Village furniture maker and magic instructor to girls who possess the gift of magic in the village of Fairendale. Is a bit reckless but always manages to come out all right on the other side—though one is not always assured it will be so.

**Maude:** Arthur's wife. Bakes spectacular pumpkin spice sugar cookies. Prefers caution to reckless abandon.

**Hazel:** Daughter of Arthur and Maude, twin of Theo. Cares for the village sheep and can even, amazingly, understand them. 12 years old.

**Theo:** Son of Arthur and Maude, twin of Hazel. Finishes his chores early so he can sit in on magic lessons. 12 years old. (Also known as the Huntsman, after a complicated Transformation spell turned him five years older and much ruddier than before.)

**Mercy:** Red-haired daughter of Cora, best friend of Hazel. Prefers spectacular acts of magic to "boring" ones.

**Cora:** Mother of Mercy, widow, sorceress, shape shifter with the form of a blackbird. A woman who moves. Unofficial leader of the village people in Fairendale who falls in and out of favor with them. Has become a dragon rider and somehow misplaced most of her magical powers.

**Garron:** The town gardener. Talks to plants as though they can hear him.

**Bertie:** The town baker. Enjoys showing off his air-kneading skills for the children—or used to. There is no longer much wheat with which to bake anymore.

## Staff of Fairendale Castle

**Garth:** Page for King Willis, the oldest of twelve children. No longer calls King Willis "Your Wideness" when he is feeling particularly prickly, because he knows how dishonoring it is to call names.

**Cook (Mira):** One of the few shape shifters in the land. Shape shifts into a bear. Is highly annoyed by her assistant, Calvin—but not really.

**Calvin:** An orphan who began working as Cook's assistant after his parents died in a Fire Mountain eruption in Ashvale. He is the only one allowed through the magical door to the dungeons beneath the dungeons and so is tasked with feeding the prisoners and keeping them alive.

**Sir Greyson:** Captain of the king's guard. Receives medicine, which keeps his mother alive, for his service to the king. Carries a magical sword that cannot be lifted by any but him—and is the only sword that can kill a shape shifter.

**Sir Merrick:** Second in command to Sir Greyson. Has a blind daughter named Agnes. Disappeared in dragon fire when crossing the lands of Morad. Presumed dead.

**Gus, Timmy, Florence:** Three blind, talking mice. Not technically staff of the castle, but they roam about it unseen, gathering information. It is suggested they were once people, transformed by a spell.

## Important Prophets

**Aleen:** Prophetess from the kingdom of White Wind who lived one hundred forty-three years. Wears ebony skin and what appears to be snakes for hair (though it is not). Sacrificed her life to change the fate of the Fairendale children in Book 6.

**Yerin:** Prophet who is one hundred forty-two years old, from the wild woodland between Lincastle and Eastermoor. Has white hair that makes the dark of the dungeons where he is imprisoned a bit less dark.

**Folen:** Former prophet of Lincastle, father of Iddo. Trapped in a looking glass created by Queen Marion. It was left on the grounds of Fairendale, just before the Great Battle.

**Iddo:** Prophet of Lincastle, son of Folen. Trained King Sebastien in both dark and light magic, though he is more scientist than sorcerer. Created a machine that can bring the dead to life again. It has only worked once.

**Bregdon:** Prophet of White Wind. Most powerful prophet in the land, known as the Old Man. Wrote and enchanted the Old Man's Great Book. Brought Queen Marion and the three Graces back to life. Lives life after life after life in a seemingly everlasting way.

## Dragons of Morad

**Zorag:** King of the dragons of Morad. Wears green scales with an ivory belly. Lost his parents in the Great Battle, when King Sebastien stole the throne from the

Good King Brendon. Would like nothing more than peace.

**Blindell:** Zorag's cousin, raised as the dragon king's son. Wears black scales and spikes all down his back. Lost his parents in the Great Battle, when King Sebastien stole the throne from the Good King Brendon. Would like nothing more than revenge.

**Larus:** One of the elder dragons of Morad, male. Counselor to Zorag. Wears blue-green scales that shimmer like water. Has a green horn on the top of his snout.

**Malera:** One of the elder dragons of Morad, female. Counselor to Zorag. Wears bright red scales and an ivory belly.

**Alvah:** One of the elder dragons of Morad, female. Counselor to Zorag. Ancient dragon who has been alive since before Zorag's father was born. Wears orange scales that used to be red but have faded in time.

**Oned:** One of the elder dragons of Morad, male. Counselor to Zorag. So ancient he is gray, colorless, with scales peeled off in places.

**Kohar:** Ancient food gatherer for the dragons of Morad, male. Wears pale yellow scales.

## Other Important Dragons

**Rezedron:** King of the dragons of Eyre, uncle of Zorag. Dying of wounds sustained from a poisonous rose in Rosehaven, believed to be dark magic.

**Nischal:** Rezedron's daughter. Unlikely to become queen of the dragons of Eyre, because of a law that forbids a female to inherit the throne.

## Residents of the Violet Sea

**Arya:** Twelfth daughter of King Tritanius, who rules the Violet Sea. Adventurous, impulsive, often considered rebellious by her father. Saves the Huntsman from death by fairy magic. Loves a mortal.

## Other Important Characters

**The Graces:** Formerly mortal women who died and were brought back to eternal life by the Old Man. Now known as Splendor, Good Cheer, and Mirth, or, collectively, the Graces. Maintain the balance of good and evil in the realm. Cannot predict the future; can only influence it.

**The Grim Reaper:** Master of the dead. Leads an army of Black-Eyed Beings. Longs to be seen as something more than a passing shadow.

**Yasmin:** Frankenstein-like creature brought back to life by the scientific tools of Iddo. Formerly known as Gladys, mother of Sebastien (future king of Fairendale, but not in her lifetime).

# The lost 12-year-old children of Fairendale

Ursula

Chester

Charles

Thumbelina (known as Lina among the children)

Minnie

**Jasper:** Transported to the land of White Wind by Hazel's Vanishing spell. Becomes a wolf who befriends a girl in a red cloak. Runs very fast.

Frederick

**Ruby:** Transported to the land of Rosehaven by Hazel's Vanishing spell. Becomes an old woman who meets Rapunzel, befriends her, and supplies her with chamomile. She is a masterful gardener.

Martin

**Oscar:** Transported to the land of Lincastle by Hazel's Vanishing spell. Remains exactly the same, even down to the holes in his boots. Loves to read, steals food by pretending to be a bird, and befriends a princess (he would never admit it is, more precisely, a crush).

**Homer:** Transported to the land of Rosehaven by Hazel's Vanishing spell. Becomes a dwarf who can spin straw into gold, otherwise known as Rumpelstiltskin.

**Anna:** Transported to the land of Eastermoor by Hazel's Vanishing spell. Becomes an old, bent woman who resides in the Were Woods. Is awkward with magic, which causes some unexpected problems.

Aurora

**Rose:** Transported to the land of Eastermoor by Hazel's Vanishing spell. Wants to be a scribe but has parents who want her to become a princess. Befriends Rose-Red and helps her fight off woodland monsters for a time.

Edgar

Harriet (known as Hattie among the children)

Isabel (known as Izzy among the children)

Ralph

Dorothy

Julian

Tom Thumb

**Philip:** Transported to the forest outside Lincastle by Hazel's Vanishing spell. Becomes the leader of the Merry

Men, otherwise known as Robin Hood. Can shoot an arrow straight to the target, even if the arrow is crooked.

## Other lost children of Fairendale

**August:** One of the lost boys of Fairendale, escaped with Theo. Known as the leader of the lost boys. Resides in a rundown shelter in Lincastle. 11 years old.

**Leopold:** One of the lost boys of Fairendale, escaped with Theo. Resides with August and the other lost boys. 11 years old.

**Fineas:** One of the lost boys of Fairendale, escaped with Theo. Formerly resided with August and the other lost boys, but was captured by the fairies of Never Land. 11 years old.

**Norman:** One of the lost boys of Fairendale, escaped with Theo. Resides with August and the other lost boys. 10 years old.

**Henry:** One of the lost boys of Fairendale, escaped with Theo. Resides with August and the other lost boys. 10 years old.

**Ernest:** One of the lost boys of Fairendale, escaped with Theo. Resides with August and the other lost boys. 10 years old.

**Agnes:** Daughter of Sir Merrick, trapped in the

dungeons beneath the dungeons of Fairendale castle. Blind, but quite good at hearing and sensing what others cannot.

# About the Author

L.R. has never won a beauty contest, been marked to marry a prince (though she did end up marrying a prince without a throne), or been urged by her mother to protect her face from the ravages of time so as to preserve her beauty, she has felt, often, the burden of a beauty-obsessed society and the opinions it has about those who don't measure up. She has, in the past, fallen for its traps, stumbled a time or two, and emerged from the fray proclaiming to every girl she knows: You are strong. You are kind. You are brilliant. You are courageous. And you are loved for being you.

She knows how much they—and she, too—need those words.

When she is not reminding girls—and boys—of their worth that has nothing to do with outward appearance, L.R. likes to read stories about strong girls, sensitive boys, and expectations turned on their head; pull out her scribe's pen and write more imaginative stories; and eat the food her king usually prepares for his family, which does not (yet) include insects.

She lives with her king and six young princes in San Antonio, Texas.

www.lrpatton.com

# A Note From L.R.

Dear Reader,

I am no stranger to the damaging ways unrealistic expectations can tell an erroneous story about who we are; that is part of the reason I am so passionate about telling a story like this one: I spent years of my life sorting through the messages a young girl absorbs in a society that says what she looks like has everything to do with her potential and opportunities in life. And though we may not be able to change the societal expectations that make girls all over the world forget who they are (or not so easily, at least), we *can* change how we allow ourselves to be limited by them.

So here is some important truth:

You matter.

You do not have to be anyone other than who you are —because who you are is enough.

You are loved simply because you are you.

I hope you always remember that. And if you forget, I will remind you—through my letters, through my musings, through my stories. I believe in the power of stories to inspire, inform, multiply love, and effect real change in the lives of readers. And I write every book with this (noble, I hope) purpose in mind.

Though my writing is done alone, my world-changing is not. I need readers like you to help get my books into the hands of those who don't yet know the hope and inspiration that can be found in them. So here are some ways you can help:

**1. Leave a review on Amazon.**

Reviews help other readers find my books. The more readers who find my book, the better I am able to accomplish what I've listed above.

**2. Tell your friends about this book.**

Word of mouth is one of the most powerful tools we have for sharing the things we love—and it is, consequently, one of the most powerful tools I have for sharing my work with new readers. Your word of mouth, spread to others.

I appreciate anything you do to help my books get into the hands of readers so that love can expand and surround and make its everlasting mark.

In love,

L.R.

# Acknowledgements

To be successful, a writer needs a team of people huddled around them, cheering them on, lifting them from the pits, reminding them who they are and why the world needs their words. My team includes, but is not limited to:

Ben, who read early drafts and raised important questions that helped me shape the manuscript into what it is today.

My sons, who listened to every word of the read-aloud sessions with rapt attention—and particularly Asa, who said, "This is *so* good." It's impossible to say what your words mean to me.

Rebecca Quint, who said, multiple times, that she can't wait until I'm famous someday and so communicated my potential (even if it never happens).

Mom, who alway asks, as soon as she's finished with one Fairendale book, "When can I read the next one?"

Kathy Ellen Davis, who is the most supportive writer friend I've ever had.

The Grimm brothers, who told such gruesome, period-specific stories I couldn't help but ask the necessary questions to write my own.

# Enjoy more stories from the magical Fairendale series:

LRPatton.com/Fairendale

# Starter Library

## A singular obsession. A safe hiding space. A never-ending search.

The king's guard has been searching all the lands of the realm for the missing Fairendale children. But, alas, Captain Sir Greyson has returned, after many days, to report to King Willis that no children have been found. The king, quite angry at this disappointing news, orders another search, this one closer to home—right inside the dangerous Weeping Woods.

*Continue your journey into the world of Fairendale with Book 2: The King's Pursuit, a short story prequel, "The Good King's Fall" and some important bonus material, **free for a limited time.***

## To get your FREE bonus materials, visit *
## LRPatton.com/goodking

*Must be 13 or older to be eligible

www.ingramcontent.com/pod-product-compliance
Lightning Source LLC
Chambersburg PA
CBHW050345190726
48284CB00007BB/2152